Zon Zombie

By DW Beam

Published in the USA in 2018 by
DW Beam Publishing,
King, NC

ISBN: 978-1-943-455-14-0

Cover Design by DW Beam
Edited by DW Beam Publishing

Author's email: dwbeam@dwbeampublishing.com

Prologue

Sitting there. Rocking backward and forward. I was a prisoner of my own device. A small room walled in. Aluminum foil on every wall, the ceiling, the floor. Lights. Everywhere. Hundreds of them. Five gallon buckets. Lights hanging right over them. Every kind of plant. Fruits, vegetables, herbs, trees, and a couple of other things as I sat there staring at the lettuce. Not as luxurious as a hotel, but it was a quick set up. You see, I turned state's evidence just three week before.

There I was, just minding my own business as usual. Had some dirty dealings with the mob. Most decent folk call them the underground terror. After being forced to do a few dirty deeds, you know, a shake down or two, just to put fear in those that owed them money, that's when a black car pulled up.

They lowered the window down. "Get in." The back door opened.

"Why should I?"

"Because I don't want to get out and beat you to a pulp." That's when he flapped out a badge and said, "And on top of that, take you to jail."

I hopped in the car. The one on the driver's side in the back seat with me began to grill me. "You are going to tell us everything you know."

"Yeah, and lose my life to the terror? No, thanks."

That's when he opened his jacket. A .44 Magnum. Big and ugly, the most powerful handgun in the world. "What about losing your life to me? How do you know I won't kill you?" he said with a deep voice.

"You don't understand. The terror don't just kill you. They kill you after they kill your family and friends, execute 'em right before your eyes. Oh, and your death, it's slow and painful. So you want to kill me? Go ahead. Kill me," I said back with an even deeper voice.

The driver looked back and said, "Look, you help us by turning state's evidence, and we'll put you under the witness protection program. I got just the guys. True one hundred percent bodyguards."

"Yeah, who's that?"

"These two guys here," he answered as he pointed to the guy in the passenger seat and mumbled his name. Then, he shook his thumb to the guy in the backseat. "Oh yeah, the tough guy back here, that's..."

Before he could get the word out, a horn blew in front of him and following the van in front of him too close at a high speed almost ended up in disaster. When the van pulled over in the left lane just in time to expose the stopped car in the right lane, he locked the brakes down just in time to go into a side skid. The cars behind us began to wreck one after another. The car spun around three times, coming to a dead stop facing the opposite way.

The driver turned around again and said, "Look, if you come with us right now, we'll not only protect you to the trail, but these two guys will stick around you long after we get your name and identity changed."

"Yeah, what are you going to be doing?" the passenger asked him.

"Well, I'm going to be overseeing the whole operation."

"How's that?" I asked.

"Oh, it's simple. I'm going with you."

Well, that's how I ended up there, staring at lettuce, rocking backward and forward.

The guy that threatened me with the gun walked into the room and said, "This needs water."

"Then why don't you water it? Why don't you act like a teacher and show me how to do it?"

"A...B...C...," he said.

I said, "A...B...C...what's that mean?"

He looked at me like he had done something great and said, "Look, I done taught you your ABC's."

"You sure are a smart teacher," I said with a smirk.

It had been three long months, and I had picked on these detectives almost as much as they picked on me. We were certainly tired of each other. The investigation didn't go at all how they had planned. The court date had been postponed twice due to certain deaths, the judge falling dead out in the parking lot and then the D.A. falling dead, both with heart attacks.

I had had enough. I couldn't take it anymore. I said, "This is not living."

"Sit down and be quiet," the detective said.

"I'm leaving."

"You ain't going nowhere."

"Yeah, the only way you're gonna stop me is to shoot me."

"Listen, we've been through this. You gotta sit tight. We're working this thing out."

I grabbed the doorknob. That's when he grabbed my arm. Big mistake. The other one stood behind him, but when I hit his jaw, his head hit the other one in the face. It knocked 'em out. They were out cold. One fell on top of the other one. I grabbed him by the coat to pull him off. It would've surely killed the other one had I not, being how big he was and all. Fat ain't the word for it.

I went out the door. As soon as I got out the door, the main detective that was the overseer pointed his gun right at my head. "Don't move an inch. Did you kill my buddies?"

"They're alright."

"I'm surprised you got the drop on 'em like you did."

"They ain't the first I got the drop on."

"Well, I won't give you the chance to get the drop on me. Now you ease back in that house or so help me, I'll put a bullet in your head."

I looked him right in the eye. "You're gonna have to 'cause I ain't going back in that house."

He pulled the hammer back. "I won't ask again."

As quick as I could, I picked up my hand and pushed the gun to the side. It went off right beside my ear. I felt the heat of the bullet as it whizzed by my head. With my hand still pushing the gun, I kicked him as hard as I could between the legs. He raised up off the ground. I had never kicked anybody so hard. He went down to the ground in a ball while I held onto his gun. He turned red in the face. It must have hurt so bad he couldn't breathe.

"Witness protection," I said right before he passed out. "Some protection. The next time I see you, I'll kill all three of you. Because as far as I'm concerned, you're all just a bunch of dirty cops, all three of ya."

And as it turned out, they really were. Witness protection. It wasn't too long until I found out the truth. The three detectives were working for the mob boss. They didn't have to kill me, but they kept me underground where I couldn't do anything. I swore if I ever saw them again that would be the last time.

1

Now, somebody's got a gun to my temple and is pressing my head to the right as sweat pours down my face. "This is it for you," the one with the gun says as he pulls the hammer back on the pistol. "Oh yeah, the boss said to make sure you see it coming."

He backs me up three feet, but on top of the eighty year old building, the forty year old air conditioner has been leaking for a while and the leak has caused four inches of water on the roof, which is now heavier than the roof can hold. The whole building begins to shake. Pieces of the ceiling fall on the gunman's head.

"What tha...?!?! The building is collapsing!" the gunman yells. "And you'll be staying here!" he finishes as he turns to walk away, looking back and pointing the gun in my direction as he goes. Just then, the air conditioner falls through the roof, crashing down on the gunman and the stairwell, leaving a big hole from the tenth floor down to the first one.

The cold sweat has now soaked my entire body. "Did that just happen?" I ask myself. "Did this building just save my life?"

The water pours for ten minutes from the roof down to the first floor. I lean over and look down. The first floor is now flooded. That's when the door behind me opens up and reveals a fire escape through a window in the back bedroom. The glass panes fall out of the window down to the floor as if the building is inviting me to a way out. "Did that just happen?" I think in my mind.

I quickly walk over to the bedroom window, still wringing wet from the sweat. I walk right out of the window onto the fire escape. As I look over, I say, "Whoa! I didn't realize I was this high up. Ten stories. I better be careful." I start down the fire escape down each flight of stairs down to the fifth floor. I'm in a hurry, but I'm exhausted. Then, the old building lets go of the fire escape from the fifth floor down.

Meanwhile, the mob boss sees me from across the street. "Would you look at that?!?" he says to his mobster gang. "That idiot couldn't even kill him! Get in there quickly!"

The mob boss sits there for a moment and thinks, "If you want things done right, well...," he jerks the handle to the door open. "Yu gotta do it yourself," he says as he walks across the street and enters into the building.

The three would be mobster gang members enter into the building first. When they open the door, water goes everywhere, knocking the third one down as the other two go on in. They go up the steps very quickly, but there are no more stairs. They will have to find another way, and they are only on the second floor.

The other mobster goes to the back after struggling through ten floors of debris all stacked up on the first floor.

The dust has not even cleared the air yet when the mob boss enters the building. His gang is out of sight, but there he stands in two inches of water. He sees the elevator shaft on the left. Standing in front of the shaft, he sees a big pile of debris in back of him and steps that only go to the second floor to the right of him. He looks back to the left. The elevator doors are ripped off, and the elevator is one floor down below the basement. Then he sees the ladder on the side of the wall going upward. It goes up six floors, and then it is torn all to pieces up there. He puts his hands on the nasty ladder that has black grease on it. After taking one look at his hands, he thinks that he might as well climb the ladder way. He is already greased up now anyway, so he begins to climb. But after reaching the third floor, the ladder bolts give way, so he has to get off at the third floor.

Now here I stand, the fifth floor, wondering if there is another way down. The fire escape is out, and going back up is no way either. As fast as I can, I take my outer shirt off, revealing a clean white t-shirt. "Ah, that's better," I think to myself. "Now, let's figure a way out of this place. Come on, old building, don't let me down."

That's when the floor underneath me, a twenty feet section falls on one end. Down to the hallway beneath, I slide right into it. Not believing what has just happened, when I stand to my feet, I look back up at the big hole in the ceiling.

Fourth floor. Shots go off, two or three. I move back just in time to miss a bullet. It is the mob boss down on the third floor, shooting up through the big hole, or what used to be two floors. "Only two more shots," I think to myself.

The mob boss stands there, probably thinking he better make this one count. I stick my head out, and the mob boss takes careful aim. He pulls the trigger as the hammer goes down on the head of the cartridge. The bullet ignites inside of the barrel as the compression zooms it out at its maximum force, the bullet straight and true. But I pull back just in time as the bullet whizzes by my head. "Wow, that was a close one, only one more shot."

I jump back out and jump back in as the mob boss shoots off the last shot. I run down what is left of the hallway on the side of the wall and then run down the other way until I get around to where I am on top of the mob boss and begin to jump up and down. And sure enough, the floor gives way. I go down right on top of the boss, at least that's what I think.

When the dust has cleared, he's standing over me with the gun. "This is it for you." He pulls the trigger. Click. Click. Click Click. Nothing happens.

I pick up one of the bricks that I fell on top of and throw it at the mobster's head. That's it for him. His eyes roll back in his head as he hits the ground. He's dead. I see a hand sticking up out of the rubble. And a foot, totally away from where the hand is. It's the other two. The old building has crushed down on top of them, killing both of them.

"The old building saved my life," I say to myself. "It was the building that killed the mob boss, too. Now all I've gotta do is figure out how those other two got up to this floor, and I'll take the easy way out. There it is. Not as easy as I thought, but that's okay. At least I'm outta here. Finally, at last, the first floor, the beautiful doors," I think. As I go out onto the street and approach the yellow lines, I hear the building groan as if it is gonna miss me and is giving its final goodbyes. As I walk to the sidewalk across the street, the building comes crashing down in one unique pile, killing the last of them and covering up everything that has just happened and any evidence of them ever being there.

In the midst of the crashing and the crumbling of the building, the mob boss' keys are spit across the road, right at my feet. I look up the road a bit at the fine car the mob boss drove, and with the new shiny keys down at my feet and no one to report the car stolen or to report the car at all, I think to myself, "I'll just borrow these keys for a while, and the car that goes with them."

2

I get in the fine Cadillac and drive off, but little do I know that two blocks down, there are two hitmen, and they are out to get the mob boss. Here they come, creeping up on the speeding Cadillac. The passenger sticks his hand out of the window with a .357 ready to shoot. Just then, a state trooper passes them by. The gunman pulls his arm in just in time to hide the gun. The state trooper turns around, and as they follow the Cadillac, the trooper pulls in on the highway. It is two lanes going and two lanes coming. The Cadillac is in the right lane.

The state trooper gets behind the gunmen and turns the lights on. The driver pulls out a silencer and puts it on a nine millimeter. It's a Makarov. "Quick shot to the temple," he thinks to himself as he pulls the car over.

As he screws the tip in, the trooper goes around him to stay behind the Cadillac. The cop sees the driver's face as he passes them and calls for backup. Another state trooper pulls up behind him as he comes up behind me.

He walks up to the car. "License, please."

After I hand him my license, he says, "You're Zon, Zon Zombie?"

"Yeah," I answer.

"Why's there blood on your t-shirt, Mr. Zombie? Oh my God, you've been shot!"

He turns around and looks at the two hitmen as they get back on the road. They do a u-turn, burning a black mark trying to get away from him. He motions to the trooper behind him. "Get after them!" he yells as he runs to his car and the other trooper races off.

After getting in his car and on his way, he sees his trooper friend run off the road. He was hit by a .357, one shot to the head. The hitman wasn't playing around.

When the trooper sees this, he races as fast as he can. Now the state trooper's car is hopped up quite a bit. It has six hundred horsepower, high compression, from zero to one hundred at the mere mash of the gas, and with that kind of force and power, he stomps his foot to the floor. And at speeds like that, no matter how accurate you are, it's gonna be hard to get a shot off.

The hitman looks up, and before he can do anything, the state trooper hits him right in the backend, snapping the passenger's neck instantly on impact, forcing both of them off the road into a big oak tree. Both cars blow up, burning everything to ash. Everyone involved is dead.

After waiting a few minutes, I think to myself, "I don't guess they're coming back." So I ease out onto the road. Where I want to go and where I need to go are two different places, and they are ten miles apart. Where I want to go is home, but where I need to go is to settle up. But with my blood stained t-shirt, I take it off and wrap it around my arm and then throw my outer shirt back on.

Suddenly, a little ding goes off. The gas tank is empty. "I better get some gas," I say out loud as if there is someone listening. I pull into a filling station. I get out and start pumping the gas.

That's when a big fella walks up, pokes me right in the ribs, and grabs me under my arm. "You're coming with us."

"Us?"

The other guy grabs me under the other arm. "Yeah, us."

A black van pulls up, and they throw me in. The big guy gets in on the passenger's side, and the scary guy gets in with him. Why scary? Well, with a scar going down his face and halfway through his ear all the way around to his back, and it isn't just any scar. It is raised up, especially around the eye, almost three quarters of an inch. With that and the particular way he carries himself, it makes him very intimidating. But not to me.

"What's this about?" I ask.

"You just sit there and be quiet. If I want you to know what it's about, I'll tell ya."

After a few minutes of driving, they pull into a big building outside of the city. The big door shuts as the van pulls up onto a ramp and an elevator lifts the van and all to the top floor.

Scary pulls out his gun. "Okay, out the door, you! Start

walking!"

It is the fourth floor of a great big warehouse building. The whole floor is empty except for a chair not too far from the middle and not too close to any window, as if it would do any good if somebody wanted to do some hurting.

"Oh no, not another building," I think to myself.

"Sit down!" the big man says.

Out of the shadows, he steps up. "I hear you owe so and so a lot of money. Three point two million to be exact. I like the way you took out those hitmen. They just disappeared. I'll tell you what I'm gonna do. I'm gonna do you a big favor. You don't owe the money no more."

"Yeah, why's that?"

"Listen, Zombie, if a man loans you money and the man is no longer living, then you don't have to pay that man back, do you?"

"Is that the case?"

"Yeah, that's the case, and I figure, well, I can kill two birds with one stone. You scratch my back, and I scratch yours. Well, I'm through scratchin' yours."

"Oh, I get it, a favor for a favor. Is that why you had your thugs pick me up?"

"I prefer to think of them as associates."

"Okay, your associates. Is that why you had them pick me up?"

"I had them pick you up because I figure you owe me a favor."

"What kinda favor?"

"Something I can't do myself. But you, being Mr. Zombie, the word is you can't die."

"Yeah, who's giving the word?"

"Ah, a few of the guys here and there. You been shot, stabbed, hung. They say you really live after your name, Mr. Zombie," he says as he breaks out with a big laugh, hardly believing what he's uttering himself.

"Okay, you've had your fun. Now what's the game? What do you want me to do?" I ask him.

"The Russians over in Short Town came over here and kidnapped my daughter. They sent me something by an anonymous carrier, something I won't disclose to you, but it's proof enough that they got her."

"So you want me to waltz over there to Short Town, waltz in, get your daughter, and waltz back out over to here."

"No, I don't want you to waltz at all, Mr. Zombie. I want my daughter back."

"Okay, I guess it's for a good enough cause. Why don't you send your own men over there?"

"I sent ten men. They didn't come back."

"Oh yeah, I'll be needing a car."

"Yeah, the boys'll handle that. Give Mr. Zombie a ride wherever he wants to go."

After getting in the van and getting well on the way, after taking down instructions, they drop me off at my house. Another man pulls up, gets out and hands me the keys to his car, and then jumps in the van.

"Just a quick shower," I think to myself. "Where's my gun?" I think as I dry off from a quick shower. I search through the drawers, then I remember, in the closet, hanging on a nail inside of the wall. "I hid it so well, I almost hid it from myself. Imagine that."

As I ponder on every little detail of what happened earlier, I can hardly believe it as I go through it step by step. It's as if the old building saved my life. Still wondering if I have imagined it, the actual way it happened.

After getting ready, I take my hand and slide it through my hair once or twice, looking at the keys in my hand as I walk down the steps. After quickly getting on the way, I pull the clip out of my nine millimeter Makarov. Six shots, two clips oughta be enough. There is another old saying going around. One shot Zombie. One shot, one kill. I never miss.

I pull up to an abandoned building and drive through the center of it very slowly. After a couple of minutes, I reach the other side of the building, come out, go down a ramp inside a newer building, and then up a ramp. The second floor, no doubt. There are a couple of cars here already. It is a small parking lot. It could hold twenty, maybe twenty-five cars, but today it only holds a few as I pull into one of the parking spots.

Sweat pouring from me once again. If nothing else, to let me know that I'm alive. I take my outer shirt off as I often do before I enter into a fight, especially if it is to the death, and at this point, I don't care if I make it out alive or dead because this time, it is for a purpose, not like before.

I step out of the vehicle and step to the back, looking for anyone. That's when off the air condition vent that overstands the cars over the particular parking space that I am in, somebody jumps right on top of me.

"Snap! His neck is broke. He goes to the ground like a sack of potatoes," at least that's what my offender thinks.

I lay there for a second, wondering what just happened. Then I realize somebody has just jumped on my back. I look up. "Ah, a rusky."

"What'd you call me?"

"A rusky."

The offender lifts up his foot and kicks me right in the mouth, only to realize that he missed. I quickly hit the side of his calf with my fist, and before he can even move his leg to let it down, I have done hit him again, lightning fast, shattering the bone.

My would be offender pulls out a knife and falls on me with the knife pointing down from his chest, clutching it as tight as he can with both hands. He can feel it go into my chest and says, "I might have a broke leg, but you've got nothing."

My eyes go cold and they wax dim, and that's when I realize I don't feel the pain any longer. I look back at my offender, grab him, and throw him off as I pull the knife out of my chest. Then I am able to get to my feet. "I don't think I like your attitude. Now I'm gonna give you a chance to tell me where the girl is," I tell him.

"Oh, I'll tell you where the girl is alright. You just get on that elevator right there, go up to the fourth floor. When you get to the end of the hall in the big room, you'll find the little girl there. Only she ain't so little. She's twenty-four years old. She's done been around a time or two if you know what I mean. But getting to her is another thing. Because you still you gotta go through me," he says as he stands up on one foot, hopping around trying to keep his balance.

He pulls out a gun. But I'm quicker. I already have my nine millimeter out and am ready to shoot, and before he can even point the gun at me, I have shot him right in the eye. His head flops back a foot and then jerks his body back slightly. It doesn't even try to straighten back up. It drops to the floor. Like cold slate dropped from the canyon walls into the water.

After pressing the elevator up button, the door bell rings. The elevator doors open. There are three men, machine guns with shoulder straps that hang down by their sides. One pulls back the action. As the bullet enters into the chamber, I have already put a bullet in his head and did the same thing to the other guy.

One left standing. "Where's the girl, and I won't ask you twice?" I tell him.

He thinks he can out speed me, and he jerks the machine gun up, pressing the trigger while he is doing it. I jump off the wall over the top of the machine gun and kick the machine gun with him behind it up against the wall. His hand gets in the way of the fire. It shoots it all to pieces. With my foot up against his chest, pressing the foot firmly up against him, I lift my gun up again and shoot him.

I start to mash the fourth floor button, but before I can push the button, the fourth floor light comes on. That can only mean one thing. The elevator is being summoned by someone on the fourth floor. I get back into the corner and change the clip out. Only six shots. And only one in the chamber. The elevator doors open, and as it cracks open one inch, I have already shot three of them. By the time it opens five inches, I have shot two guys and karate chopped the one that mashed the button one time across the shoulder right at the neckline. It breaks his neck. Then, three other guys come out of a little room off to the side, just to add to the fatalities.

With one bullet left in the magazine, I quickly assess that the girl isn't there. That's when I hear a gun go off from across the room. I look down at my white t-shirt. It was already red from the knife wound that should have killed me, but now I am bleeding from another spot, a gunshot wound.

The assailant jumps up and shoots twice again and reaches for a two inch piece of conduit on the wall to climb up to the next floor. It is rack flooring. You can see through it, but when he gets to the top, over to where he can jump to the landing, the conduit gives way. It is loaded with two seventy voltage. When that conduit cuts into that wire, it takes two hundred straight amps through him down to the ground. It instantly burns his hand right off, and with his other hand touching the railing, his elbow blows up on his other arm, leaving nothing but a stub. As he jumps, his head catches the sharp edge, ripping him open. He is hardly recognizable after he hits the ground.

"Well, I know not to go that way," I say out loud, looking down at my gun shot wound, wondering to myself what has just happened. "Is this building trying to save me, too?" I tell the old building, "Save the girl." But I laugh in disbelief.

I climb up to the balcony and walk across the room. Over to the right is an office. I listen very closely. A shot goes off, and a bullet comes through the door. I go for the doorknob, but it is locked. I kick the side of the doorknob, but it is no use. It's a steel door. It opens to the inside.

Another shot goes off. After backing off and assessing the situation, a little ways down the hall is a maintenance room. It has a bolt lock on it and a lock on the doorknob. "How am I gonna get into here?" I wonder to myself. I reach and turn the doorknob. It opens right up. A maintenance man works on everything from the furnace to the air conditioner on the roof. It is pretty obvious. He has every tool there is. And inside the maintenance room is an elevator, obviously to get to the tools and get to the main floor and the top floor with easy access.

I see a blue rope, three quarters of an inch thick. "Ah, that's nice," I think to myself as I pick it up and throw it over my shoulder with my head toward the middle. I take the elevator two floors up, come out of the other hall, and go into the room two stories up from where I am trying to get in. There is a big glass window inside of the room. It is a bigger room. It doesn't have a hallway, but it is still over the room I am needing to be in.

I take a desk and push it as hard as I can right out of the window right onto the street. "So much for surprise," I yell out as I tie the rope around a beam that is in the middle of the floor all the way across the room. I let the end of the rope down to where the floor is and then pull it back up, use it to measure with, and then tie it off. Then I let myself down to right on top of the window and kick as hard as I can. As soon as I do, I let the rope down six feet which places me right in the middle of the glass.

Boom! Right in the middle. It doesn't move. By this time, everybody's attention is on the glass and me on the outside of it with all guns pointing toward me. As soon as I see them pointing guns at me, I kick off again. They let it go as I pull myself up the rope and bounce back up to the top to the rim of the window.

Now with everybody in the room shooting, the glass is gone. It has fallen to the road. I kick off the edge again and drop back down. As soon as the firing stops, "It's reload time," I think to myself. "Now it's my turn."

I let go of the rope as I fly in through the window. The first one reloads, an automatic machine gun. All he has to do is change out the clip, pull back the action, and fire away. And that's exactly what he does. But not one shot hits me. It hits the floor beside me where I slide across, and a few bullets whiz across my face.

With one bullet, I let it go. By the time the shooter gets through firing, the second one is reloaded and ready to shoot. A .45 auto, Smith and Wesson. He drops the clip out and places another one in there. "If I get hit with one of those," I think to myself, "well, it won't be good."

He aims down toward the floor as I get up off the floor, jump across a table to where the machine gunner is, and shoot through a chair with the machine gun. A bullet hits me in the leg. I look behind me. Another guy with a .357, he is already half loaded, a revolver.

By this time, all of them have their guns loaded, the remaining five. I jump up off the ground onto my feet, grab the barrel of the .357, and jump behind the assailant, turning him around to where his back is facing the rest of the four guys. They let loose, shooting the one with the .357 right in the back. Part of his head flies off as it mystifies. By this time, he has already let go of the

21

gun. As the body falls to the floor, shot up, the two with revolvers run out of bullets again and have to reload, but the one with the . 44 and the one with the .38 revolver are a little more resourceful. As soon as that body falls out from in front of me, I take careful aim, and as quick and as fast as he is, shoot him right in the eye. That ends the automatic.

The other three see that they are outgunned. The first one to finish loading his gun looks up, and I have the gun pointed right at his head. He has just closed the cylinder to where the gun is ready to fire. I shake my head, "No, don't do it." But he tries to outgun me and falls to the floor dead.

The other one is almost through loading his gun, so I shoot him in the head. The last one standing. He drops the gun to the floor and put his hands up. "Just tell me where she is, and I won't throw you out of this window."

"You won't get nothing out of me."

I shoot him in the kneecap. "Wrong answer."

That's when somebody steps out of the side room with a gun up to her head. There is something wrong with this picture. I quickly point the gun at him. "Shoot me, she dies," he says.

But she has brown hair, blue eyes. The other mob boss told me she had blonde hair, green eyes. As I think this to myself, I shoot her right in the head. She is no doubt part of the gang. I wasn't for sure at first, but it was the little tatoo. I couldn't make it out. It was right behind her ear on her neck, just enough for me to see that it was the same tatoo the others had.

When she falls to the ground, the gunman stands there in shock. He can't believe I have shot her. That's when the other guy goes to pick up his gun. I shoot both of them. I look in the room. No girl. I search all over the building. There is no trace.

I exit the building, and there the big black Cadillac pulls up across the street. The window rolls down as I walk across the road. The blonde with green eyes sits there looking at me. The mob boss yells out, "Well done."

"Your daughter was never in danger," I say.

"Yeah, she could've been. These were other gangsters that were gonna kill you. I heard through the grapevine that they were going to take my family, and this is all I have left of my family, my daughter. Now you know I can't let them take her."

"Yeah, yeah, you can't let certain things happen, but I don't think it's got anything to do with your daughter. Let me guess. I took out all your competition."

"Now listen, Zombie, they were gonna kill you, too. You done yourself a favor. Now there's no contract out on your life."

"Yeah, I'm sure you're worried about me, and I'm sure you're worried about your daughter, too. It's just a matter of time before we cross paths again. You better be on my good side when we do."

"I'll see to it," the mob boss says as he raises up the window and drives off.

I go over to the side of the curb and sit down. I have been stabbed, shot, lacerated from falls, cuts, and bruises. I'm a mess. That's when everything goes black.

3

I wake up in a hospital. "Oh there you are." It's a beautiful young nurse. But ain't they all? "We didn't think you were gonna make it."

Unable to talk with a tube down my throat, that's when she begins to pull it out. I begin to cough and choke. I begin to moan as I grab for my chest. Twenty-three stitches. The bleeding has stopped, but the pain hasn't.

"How long have I been here?"

"Well, you're in intensive care, but after the surgery, the wounds healed up. Now that you're awake and aware, maybe we can move you to a room."

I look down at my arm, the gun shot wound. Then I look down at my leg, another gun shot wound. Then I look at the handcuffs on my wrist where the IV is.

"What's going on?"

"Well, there are officers outside. They're not allowed in intensive care."

"Why do they have handcuffs on me?"

"Well, you've been in some kind of gun fight, and there are a lot of people dead to your account."

"You've gotta help me get these cuffs off."

She looks out the door to where the cops are to see if anybody has heard me. "I can't do that."

"Why not?"

"Mainly because I'm scared to death. I've never done anything like this."

"All you have to do is get me something to get these cuffs off with."

"What do I get? I don't know what to get."

"A paperclip and a staple."

She goes back to the nurse's station and then comes back. "Here are some staples, and here's a paperclip," she says. "But how's that gonna get handcuffs off?"

I break off one of the staples and shove it in the hole. "Hold this staple here," I tell her. I use the paperclip, put it in beside of the staple, and push gently up against the clip. "Now push the staple farther in," I say, "To the side." When she does, I pull the paperclip off and the handcuffs fall off.

She looks back at the door with her hands quivering. "I'll have to use some ingenuity here," I think.

She says, "I've got an idea." She goes to the other end of the room and comes back. It's a doctor's coat and a pair of slacks that belonged to me when I came in. They have blood all over them.

"Listen, the blood's dry, and the coat will cover up the holes. Here's a stethoscope. Put these around your neck, and put these glasses on."

I pick up a clipboard from off the end of the bed. "Nurse, walk with me," I say as I head toward the door. As I open the door, I tell her, "Yeah, this patient will not last through the night. I'm surprised he isn't already dead," as we walk past the police officers that stand beside the door. "Give him twenty ccs of phenobarbitol," I say as I hand her the clipboard as she grabs for the door to shut it.

But by the time we get to the end of the hall, one of the police officers looks at the other one. "Did you see that doctor go past us?"

"Yeah, I saw him walk past us. He walked right out the door and right down the hall."

"Yeah, but did you see him go in?"

That's when the other police officer opens the door, walks into the room, and slides the curtain back. There is nothing but a blood drenched bed. "Dang it," he says. "Get after 'em!" he yells.

By then, I have already disappeared. I am long gone. No allies. No friends. Except maybe one, a double crossing mobster and his beautiful daughter. "I'll have to pay him a visit, but where will he be?"

With no gun, no identity, no wallet, and no money, I better find him fast. "Think!" I tell myself. "This is gonna take time. I got it. I'll go to the docks where the boats are coming in." After spending half the night looking for a certain dock, I think to myself, "Now what am I looking for?" This is the third dock and the last one "Oh, that's what I'm looking for, right there. Guards, with guns, in suits. Now what do you think they're doing here? I'll just walk on up."

"Hey, hold it right there," the guard says as he points his gun toward me.

"Hey, what's going on?!?! I'm just looking for a job."

"You're looking for a job in the wrong place. Now turn around and leave."

"What's going on? Why do you got a gun?"

"I've got a gun because....," he says as he pulls out a wallet with a badge in it and flaps it open to show the badge. "FBI, now hit the road! And don't make me say it again!"

"Since when do FBI agents stand guard on a dock with machine guns?"

"You don't get the point," the guard says as he puts the gun under my chin.

"Oh, I got the point alright. I'll just leave now."

The agent pulls the gun out from under my chin as I back away. I go out the gate I came in. The agent calls for other guards that are on the outside of the gate. They come through. "Hey, did you take care of him?" the guard asks.

"We never did see him."

"Nevermind, just get the shipment off the boat."

It takes about three or four hours, but finally, a big truck is loaded. It drives out the gate slowly and eases up to a stoplight. Two other cars pull off in front of it and two in the back. Then they make their way across town slowly. Now usually trucks like this at nighttime creeping through town, well, it would raise enough suspicion for a cop to investigate, and that's what one cop does, investigates it.

He gets behind the two cars in the back and puts his lights on. The one car pulls over. He passes it, and then the next car pulls over. The truck mashes the gas to go a little faster, but with the two cars in front of him, he has to pull over, too. The last car pulls up beside the officer as he steps out of the car. Well, it isn't a nice sight. They each one drive by as the truck gets back on the road and they get back into formation. It was silent and quiet, one shot.

After they get to the other side of town, there are sirens going off all over the place. When somebody gets shot in this town, nobody does anything, but when a cop gets shot, all hell breaks loose. But it's too late.

They enter into the gate. Then the doors open into the warehouse, and the truck disappears along with the cars. As cops go by with lights on, their sirens disappear into the distance. They back the truck up to an elevator and take all the merchandise off. It takes a little while. The last stack of merchandise is placed into the elevator. The big doors shut, and the elevator rises to the fourth floor.

After a long while, the door shuts again, and it goes down to the third floor. The door opens. "Boss, the shipment's all in order."

"Was there any trouble?"

"One fatality. A cop's dead."

"I kinda figured it must have been a cop with all the commotion going on. That'll be all. Let me know if there are any changes."

28

He lifts the phone back up to his ear. "You owe me about one point three billion dollars. I expect payment in the morning."

"Yeah, I got the shipment," he says to the person on the phone.

"Yeah, once a month, just like I promised. You get the money. I get the goods. Just like it's always been."

"Well, that won't be a problem," he says. "Thanks to Zombie, he won't be a problem anymore."

"Because he's dead, he and all his men. Zombie took care of it for me, and he didn't even know he was working for me."

"Okay, first thing in the morning." he hangs up the phone.

The mob boss sits there quietly for a moment, thinking. Then he asks, "How long have you been here?"

I step up into the light where he can see me. "Why'd you do it?" I ask.

"Why'd I do what, Zombie? I been right here."

"Why'd you want me to kill the other mob bosses?"

"The question is, why did you do it? You're the one that killed 'em, not me. Why all that hate and anomosity? Full of kill and murder."

"Look, don't get smart with me. You know who I am."

"I know who you are, but you won't hurt me."

"Yeah, why is that?"

"Because I know your reputation. You only hurt those that come against you or the ones you love, and up until now, I've been on your side."

"You're just a thug, like everybody else I worked for."

"Zon, what do you want? Why are you here? I thought our

business was completed on the street curb, and while you're answering that, you might wanna ask yourself why you killed the other mob boss."

"He was no good. But why'd you want him dead?"

"He was killing my men and taking my shipments. Why did you want him dead?"

"You know the score. He put a contract on me."

"Yeah, well nobody's closed that contract. If you'd like, I could shut it down."

"I don't need your help."

"Zombie, you need to come to work for me. I'll treat you right. You'll have plenty of money, plenty of prestige, and plenty of power."

"And what part of that do you think I don't have already?"

"Yeah, I guess you're right."

"Was that even your daughter in the car with you?"

"Heavens no, you think the way I look, I could have such a beautiful daughter as that. Ha ha ha," he laughed.

"Yeah, I found it pretty unbelievable myself. I'd kill you right now if I even suspected that you were going to try to take me out."

"No, on the contrary, Zombie, I feel that we need each other."

"How's that?"

"Well, I wanna live, and you can't die."

"So you wanna live through me a little, do you?"

"Well, not exactly. I just think we would make really good partners, that's all."

"I'll be leaving now."

"Why'd you come?"

"I'm not sure."

That's when his daughter, or whoever she is, walks in. "I'm going home now," she tells the boss.

"Oh, it's you again," she says, looking at me.

The mob boss calls her by name and says, "Look, Zombie needs a place to stay. Maybe you could let him stay the night at your place."

She looks at me. First at my eyes, then she looks at me all the way down to my feet as her mouth drops open and her eyes get bigger. She pants for air, trying to not be obvious about the disgust that she feels inside. She looks at the mob boss with a face that says, "Are you kidding me?"

"Now be nice to Mr. Zombie. He's a good friend of mine," he tells her.

I'm still a mess, the clothes I have had on for several days, bloody. She looks at me with disgust and says, "I guess. Come on with me."

After going down the elevator, she walks over to the dark part of the warehouse. The big doors open up, and the light shines on her car. "Are you coming?" she asks with a monotone voice.

"Yeah, I reckon," I say. "I ain't got no place else to go."

"You're not gonna kill me or anything, are you?" she asks.

"I haven't made up my mind yet."

After I get into the car, she drives out of the warehouse, out the gate, and down the road. The next block up, there are two cop cars. They have two of the mob boss' thugs as she turns down the block before it. Their car must have broken down. Otherwise, they would have never gotten caught. That's even if it is the same ones that killed the cop earlier.

After she turns off, I ask, "What's your part in all this?"

"My part?" she says. "I don't have a part."

"How'd you get tied up with the mob?"

She tells me the story. Her dad's friend owed the mob boss money. When her dad found out they were going to kill his friend because it was more than he could pay, her dad went to the mob boss and asked if he could take the debt and pay it off. He wrote out a check and gave it to the boss. It was a great deal of money.

"Is your friend worth it?" the mob boss had asked.

"He's my friend," her dad answered.

"I like you," the mob boss said. "You've got a daughter, don't you? She's what, ten, eleven, twelve years old?"

Her dad told him she would thirteen a week from that day.

"Well, since you took care of your friend," the mob boss said, "I'm gonna be your friend. If anything ever happens to you, I promise I'll take care of your daughter and make sure everything goes according to the way you would raise her. This is my promise to you."

"That was thirteen years ago," she says.

"Oh, you're twenty-six?" I ask.

"Twenty-seven."

"So that still doesn't explain why you're with the mob boss now?"

"I'm not with him. He's taken care of me for the last thirteen years."

"And?"

"You know the mob boss you killed with all his thugs in the building before you met me?"

"Yeah," I answer.

"Well, when my dad left from paying off his friend's debt, they both got in the car to leave, and right before they got two blocks from getting home, a car bomb blew up my dad and his best friend. It goes without saying that my dad's best friend also owed the other mob boss almost a million dollars. My dad didn't know about that. That's why it got 'em both killed."

"So you're the reason the big boss wanted the other boss dead? So it wasn't drugs."

"Oh, I'm sure it was drugs, too. Laundered money, guns, and anything else. He wants to take over the whole operation."

"Monopolize, huh? That's not good for a mob boss to want to have it all. He's not gonna have many friends."

"That's why he came to you," she says as we pull up to her house.

"Ah, nice house. It's not exactly a mobster's house."

"No, it's not. I went to college. I got a good job. I pay my own way."

"So it's not mob money, huh?"

"Not one red penny."

After we enter into the house, she takes me to one of the bedrooms that is empty, goes into the bathroom, and comes out, handing me a towel, a washrag, and a bar of soap. "You can start here," she says.

With blood still dripping from my head and my wounds, I say, "I'll be needing a needle and some thread." I go into the bathroom as she waits outside of the bedroom.

After two hours, she wakes up on the couch. She goes and opens the bedroom door. The bathroom door is still shut. "What is he doing?" she thinks to herself. "I guess I'll fix us something to eat."

So she goes into the kitchen and looks into the refrigerator. There isn't much there. It is because she was overseeing her daddy's killer's death that she wasn't able to get groceries the day before. She doesn't run around with the mob boss except for this one event.

He had pulled up to her house and walked into her house as if he owned it. He called her by her name and said, "Look, you need to come with me."

Terror hit her face. "Now, now, it ain't nothin' like that. I just want you to see something," the mob boss told her.

She loosened up her shoulders from being tensed that he was even there at her house and said, "What?"

He said, "I promise, you're gonna wanna see this. After this day, I'll never mess with you again, just like I promised your dad."

She had a solemn look on her face. She said, "Okay," with humility in her voice and relief to hear that he would never mess with her again.

That's when she had gotten in the car and they had parked down the road from the building that Zombie had entered in, and that's where she carefully watched the mob boss and his thugs enter into the building. She could hardly believe her eyes as smoke rolled out of the bottom of the building, and one after another one, they entered in, and after a while, Zon came out. Then she had been at the other building as she watched Zombie take out of all of the mob boss' other competition.

While remembering all this, she has thrown a steak in the frying pan big enough for the both of them, then she cuts it down the middle. It is forty-five minutes later. She throws it on the table. That's when I walk out the door. She straightens up and looks at me with a surprised look. She can hardly believe her eyes. "Wow," she says. "You really clean up nice. I hardly recognized you."

"Well, blood does disguise you quite a bit. I hope you don't mind me using your housecoat."

"That's not my housecoat."

"I thought it was kinda big when I put it on. I won't ask whose it is."

"It was my dad's."

"Oh, I thought maybe a boyfriend or a husband."

"Are you kidding me? I'm protected by one of the biggest mob bosses in the state. What kinda guy would even get a hundred feet close to me?"

"You mean besides guys like me?"

She puts a smirk on her face and says, "Exactly."

"Well, don't worry. I won't be around too long."

"What do you mean, too long?"

"I'll leave in a little while. Is that steak for me?"

"I suppose, if you're hungry. Here's some salad and a baked potato."

After I sit down and eat a steak, a potato, and a little bit of salad, she asks me, "So how long is a little while?"

"I'm not sure," I answer.

After I get through cleaning my plate out and putting it in the sink, I go over and sit on the couch. As soon as I do, I fall straight to sleep. She can't help but to feel sorry for me, so she goes over and sits beside me. She turns the TV on and falls fast asleep.

It is six o'clock in the morning, the six o'clock news. I wake up to the sound of a high pitched voice. I know that high pitched voice. I have heard her many times. "There was a shootout earlier, and the assailants got away. Be on the lookout for such and such and such and such. They are wanted for questioning for attempted murder and murder in the first degree. Three detectives were shot to death at four a.m. this morning. After a brief shootout, the wounded assailants drove away. If you see these men," she says as they show their pictures, "please get a hold of your local law enforcement. These men are armed and dangerous. Be on the lookout for them."

When I move and sit up on the couch, the young lady wakes up, too. "Well, that's it," I say.

"That's what?" she says.

"That's part of my problem right there, solved."

"What do you mean?"

"I just spent three months with those guys. They ain't no good. They deserved to die. I was gonna kill 'em myself."

"Well, ain't you glad you didn't?" she asks.

I look at her in her eyes and say, "Not really."

She moves back a little bit and says, "Well, how does this solve your problem?"

"The hitman that was hired by one of the mob's employees is the last of my problem and the only reference to me and my situation. The mob boss and his thugs that I killed and these three men here are the reason I'm in the shape that I'm in. No money, no place to go."

"Listen, Zon, the word on the street is that you can't die, so what does a hitman have to gain out of trying to kill you?"

"I only know one thing. He will try."

No sooner have I gotten those words out my mouth, it happens in slow motion. At first, I feel a vibration as I look toward the window. The glass begins to shake, and then cracks begin to spread out throughout the window, and right in the start of the cracks, a hole with glass coming out of it, coming straight for me. Then, a bullet appears.

It is coming straight for my head. I watch it in slow motion as it comes toward me, and I move my head over to the side and keep my eyes on the bullet as it goes by. Then, I put my head back into place and look out the broken glass.

It is a house across the street. A car had followed us home to her house and parked across the street. In the dark air of the morning, he got out, opened the trunk, and got out a case. He walked up to the door and rang the doorbell with his black leather gloves tightly formed to his hands. He held the case in his left hand and opened the screen door with his right hand. It was a middle aged woman, and as soon as she opened the door, well, it was silent and quick. He picked her up and put her on the couch as he shut the front door. He walked through the house and, well, there were no survivors.

When he got done with his dirty deeds, he went to the front window. He took out some pipes, screwed them together, and set them up in the living room floor. It was a heavy duty gun stand when he got through. He mounted the gun that he had put together. It was a cylinder, one foot long. He placed it over the barrel at the end. He took the scope and took careful aim through the window and into the window across the street, waiting for me to come out of the bedroom.

He took a cutting tool and cut a round circle into the picture window of the house that he was in. He moved the gun around, looked through the other window, and put a bead on her head, but she was not why he was there. He sat down in a chair, looking through the windows, waiting for me. But it had been three days since the mob boss had hired him, and he hadn't slept. Night or day. Sitting there, he fell asleep, thinking about the next kill. Me.

But when the sunlight hit the window, he could hardly stand the pain of the light hitting his eyes. He pulled the shade down right to the top of where he had cut the window out and looked through the sight. It was me, sitting on the couch. He took careful aim, right between my eyes, right at my forehead. He fired the gun. With the silencer, you would not have heard any noise at all except for when the glass broke. It was like a baseball hit it. That's when he looked back through, and there I was, looking straight at him.

The only difference is that beneath my eye is a .357 with a nine inch barrel. There is an exchange of bullets as if it is in slow motion. The bullet hits right through the hole that he had cut into the glass, right in the end of the scope, and goes right through the

38

hitman's eye and out the back of his head.

The young lady screams as she grabs her mouth with both hands. "Oh my gosh, what are you doing?!?!?"

"I'm getting rid of the rest of my problem," I tell her.

"How is that getting rid of your problem, shooting off that cannon in my house like that?"

I put my arm around her, slide her close to me, and say, "Look," as I point my .357 across the street.

She says, "I don't see nothing."

I say, "Look closer at the picture window across the street."

"There's nothing there but a pulled down blind above a circle, looks like a hole. Is that what you just did? That's impossible."

"No, that's not what I just did. That was the hitman on the other side of that hole. He won't bother us no more."

"Us? What do you mean, us? You were leaving after a little while, remember?"

"Well, has it been a little while?"

She was all uptight, but when I say that, she loosens up a little bit and kinda lets me hug her with my arm around her. "I'll let you know."

"In a little while?" I ask.

She gives me a big grin as she pulls close to me and says, "Yes, in a little while."

Almost half asleep, I sit there dazed and confused, thinking on so many things. She knows who I am, but does she know what I am?

It all started a long time ago, too long ago if you ask me. It was a local gang of teenage boys who loved to play with fire, but this time it was my block. It may have not been my building, but it was all the same to me when they went up to a roof and lit a bonfire right in the dead center of it. Now when I saw 'em coming out of the building one by one, scattering each to their own direction, that's when I looked up and saw smoke.

I ran to the top of the building as fast as I could, but by then, the flames had gotten bigger and the tar coated pebbles that were on top of a thin sheet of rubber were now at a blaze. The gang members had taken a couple of crates and then took a couple of more and sat them on top of those, then sat them on fire, obviously to burn the building down as they had done so many times before.

I ran down to the next floor. No fire extinguisher. I looked over to the other side of the hall where I thought a fire extinguisher would be, and there was a water hose. As fast as I could, I ran up to the rooftop with the water hose, then I ran down to turn the water hose on. The water didn't work. I was now exhausted. My legs were on fire. So were my lungs. I must have gotten a good whiff or two of the smoke.

"The next floor has a fire hose, too," I thought. So I went down the steps as fast as I could, and before I unrolled the hose, I turned the water on. It filled up the hose right at the end right by the faucet. I turned the water off and unraveled the hose until I got up to the roof and then I went down and turned the water on.

By this time, the wood beneath the rubber was on fire. The smoke was too much. It was blowing right where I was standing. I didn't have enough hose to pull it out onto the roof properly, so I stood there for almost twenty minutes while a little bit of water got on it at a time. But after that black tar got on fire and that rubber, there were enough carcinogens in there to choke any living being to death. Everything went black.

When I woke up, I was on the fire escape on the bottom floor. The fire was out. The smoke was gone, and I was wondering how I got there. Who saved me and why?

That's when it happened. I threw up right there on the fire escape, but what I threw up is the question. It was black. It was thicker than molasses. I must have emptied out a gallon of this stuff as it dripped down to the cement. I should have passed out because I threw up a good long while without breathing, but I didn't.

As if it were normal, I went on about my business, but that wasn't the first time I had put out a fire in one of these buildings. Still dizzy and disoriented, I climbed down the steps. That's when everything went black again.

I woke up on the cement this time, and I looked up to where I should have fallen from. I was far away from it. Somebody caught me. But where were they? Where did they go? The funny thing is, disoriented as I was, I looked up at that old building and that fire escape, and it seemed to be putting itself back on the side of the building. That's when I threw up again, another gallon of the black stuff.

"I've gotta get to a hospital," I thought to myself. I walked to the emergency room on foot. It took quite a while, but when I was fixing to walk into the hospital, I put my hands in my pockets. No insurance. No cash. I knew they wouldn't accept me. I stood there with my pockets hanging out, scratching my head, wondering why I had walked so far just to realize that it was for nothing.

Time went on. I got older, a lot older. It was almost ten years later when I watched the gang go into another building. But this time, they had guns, and there were a lot more of 'em. And they were a lot meaner, too. By this time, they had moved to bigger and better things. Little did I know it, but for the last ten years, they had been working for the mob, who would buy buildings and take insurance out on 'em, then get the local gangs to set 'em on fire.

But this time, there were members in the apartment of the building, and as I ventured up through the stairwell, here they came off the ninth floor. Now each stairwell between the floors had two staircases. One went back to the wall which had a window in it, and the next flight up went to the door for the next floor. Each floor had two flights of steps. When they saw me, I was by the window in the middle of the two floors.

I looked at them, and they looked at me. "Get him, guys," one of them said. But before I could get down two flights of steps, they were on top of me, beating me, kicking me. After I should have been dead, they stopped beating on me and went down. When they got down two flights of steps, I don't know how, but I got up off my feet and made my way to the top floor.

By the time I got to the roof, they were all on top of it. No time to hide. That's when I came up beside a big barrel of water, and before the fire could get big, I dumped that big old barrel over. No, it didn't put it out, but it put enough water underneath it where it wasn't going to burn the building.

"You're the dirty rat that's been putting out our fires, ain't ya?" the leader of the gang said.

"These buildings have a history," I said. "You should have respect for 'em instead of burning 'em down to the ground."

He pulled out a gun. "Take that," he said as he pulled the trigger. One shot after another one, but he kept missing. After six shots, he ran out. Click. "Shoot this guy, will you? What's the matter with this gun?" he said.

While he stood there loading his gun again, the others took turns shooting, one after another one. There was a cooling tower behind me. Water was going everywhere. I got to thinking, "I should be dead. They're not gonna stop shooting until I am." So I dropped to the rooftop face down with my face turned away from them.

"Go check him, will you?" the leader said.

"Yeah, he's dead alright. He's got holes all over him. There's holes going through his pants, his shirt. Nobody could have lived through that."

"Well let's get out of here, then."

"Did you see the way he just stood there?!?!?" one of them exclaimed in shock. "I must have emptied out twelve rounds into him!"

"He didn't flinch, jerk, or nothing!" another one said as they went off the roof down the stairwell. "Like a zombie!"

When I heard them echoing from the stairwell from a rooftop door, that's when I raised up, looking at my clothes. I raised my shirt up, expecting to see wounds. There were none. "I better get to the hospital," I thought to myself again, almost to the point of shock as to why I wasn't dead.

I started walking down that stairwell, and as soon as I put my hand on the stairwell banister, I could hear one of 'em down there saying, "Look, it's him." As fast as they could, one after another one, they clogged the stairwell again, and as fast as they could, they made their way up to me.

The old building began to shake as I held onto the banister. As soon as they got to the stairs of the top floor, the first section, they all stood there looking at me. They jerked out their guns again, but this time, as they aimed their guns at me, some holding on to the banister, before they could shoot again, for some unknown reason, the banister gave way.

Now in the banister section all the way down to the ground,

there was about three to four feet one way and about eight feet the other way. The whole set of steps gave out, but the flight that I was on and the floor way to the window where the fire escape was was left unharmed. As for the others, flight after flight, all the way to the ground as each one of them was left with posts sticking out of them from the banister where the beams lifted up just before each one hit.

That's when I thought, "I got a feeling this building don't like ya very much." They had burnt their last building. No one shared my experience with anybody else because there were none left living.

I climbed out of the window and went down the fire escape. But there was something different about me. As for the name, I stuck with it because I had lost my memory after being shot in the head before all this happened. I never had a last name because I couldn't remember it.

Now well in age looking back, I realize that I saved many of those old buildings. One from a bomb one time, stumbled on it by accident, but the red light was blinking, a big ol' case. It was C4. Whoever was doing this meant business. Now I didn't know how to disarm a bomb, but I knew those caps went into that C4. I just took all the caps out and moved the plastic explosives out of the case.

Yeah, them caps went off alright like a shotgun, but as far as the explosives, I've still got 'em, almost a hundred pounds of C4. It would have taken this building down easy and another one that was beside it which was probably also insured.

An anonymous letter went to all the insurance companies not

too many years ago. It simply said, "Larceny by the owner. Paid local gangs to do aiding and abetting. The proof is on the top of the buildings where they set fires which were mysteriously put out."

The insurance companies got together with the investigators, and any rooftop fires started, their insurance policies were canceled. After the owners got stuck with a few burnt buildings, the scam quickly died away, but I didn't.

5

But I had my own thing going. As long as I was in these buildings, I was invincible. Yeah, I suffered injury, but it quickly healed. But sometimes I didn't suffer at all. When I got shot in the head, I was nowhere near these buildings. Had I been, I would have been able to remember my name and where I came from. I do remember waking up from it though....

I woke up. My head was throbbing. I had missed the doctor's appointment for my head injury. They told me I was shot. I had no idea what they were talking about, but I knew I better not miss this appointment. The doctor and the nurses were the only people I knew when I woke up. Dr. Dason. Nine o'clock appointment.

As I went through town, there were certain areas where I could sense danger, but when I got to the doctor's office, it was somewhat crowded. At first, I felt fine. I heard my name, Mr.

Zon.

I stood there puzzled for a minute, wondering who they were talking about. But it was only three weeks earlier when I had woken up in the hospital. One of the nurses showed me the hat that I obviously had on when I got shot in the head. There was a bullet hole going in the side of it right through the patch. It was obviously a name brand hat, but Zon was the first part of the first word. The last part of it was shot away as the bullet went into my forehead and came out the side of my head.

"Do you remember your name?" the nurse had asked me.

But looking at the hat and seeing the word Zon, I read the word out, "Zon."

"Dr. Dason," she cried out as she threw the hat down on the bed on top of me, "he remembers his name."

Dr. Dason came into the hospital room. "So you remember your name?" he asked

"What?!? No...yes, I'm not sure."

"Doctor, he said his name was Zon," she said.

As I picked up the hat and showed it to the doctor, I said, "I guess it's Zon then, but I don't remember anything."

"You were shot in the head," he explained as he told me the story.

Now I was standing in the doctor's office waiting to be checked in so the doctor could examine the stitches he had done on my head, and pull them out of, course.

"Mr. Zon, come this way please," one of the nurses politely said to me. She weighed me in and then took me to the examining room. There I sat on the bed as the doctor took out my stitches.

"Dr. Dason, will I ever remember who I am?" I asked.

"I am afraid not, Zon. The damage was extensive. The bullet went into part of your brain. You're lucky to be alive. Has anybody claimed to know you?"

"Not yet."

"Where are you staying? What's going on with you?"

"One of your head nurses knew my dilemma, and he allowed me to stay with him for a while. I've got a job down at the car lot selling cars. I sold one today, Dr. Dason."

"Oh, that's good."

"If I sell two more, I move up to salesman, and I won't be making minimum wage anymore."

"Well, let's hope you sell plenty of them then. Now Zon, I don't want you to work hard. I want you to take it easy, give your brain a chance to heal."

"Yeah, I was hoping for some good news about my memory. Sometimes I remember things. I have the strangest dreams, and I keep having these premonitions."

"Premonitions?" the doctor asked.

I said, "Well, you know, I sense things."

"What do you mean? Explain."

"Well, I sense danger right now."

"Zon," he said as he patted me on the back, "I assure you. You're in no danger. I wouldn't hurt a fly, especially you. You're my number one patient, and I was going to tell you that if you needed a place to stay or if you need money or anything, just let me know and I'll help you get on your feet anyway I can."

"Well, Dr. Dason, that's awful nice of you and I appreciate the offer and all, but like I said, I'm working. I'll be on my feet in no time. I feel like you're the only one I know, Dr. Dason, and of course, a couple of your nurses that have been so kind to me. I can't thank you all enough. I wish I could repay you."

He opened the door and said, "I'm not going to set another appointment, but if anything goes wrong or you feel you need to see me, just come on in and I'll make room for you. You don't have to make another appointment."

"I appreciate it, Doc."

As we walked out into the hallway, someone kicked the door in. Two men entered in into the area where the nurse's station was. Machine guns. Not the cheap old ones, the real expensive new ones, the kind the military use.

That's when I said, "Military mode activated," and for some reason, I took off running. I jumped up on the banister, kicked off the banister, jumped off the wall, and kicked right into the neck of the first assailant. It was amazing. I kicked him so hard he went skidding right by the other guy as I jerked his gun out of his hand.

That's when he opened fire. He was more nervous than he was dangerous as he let it rip going across the room, trying to hit me, no doubt, but right before the bullets got to me on the floor, I had already taken careful aim right into the center of his torso and right up through his head. Five or six shots from his stomach up to his head as he went back through the busted door he had just kicked in.

Now there were two entryways and another hall. Here came two more down the other hall straight to the nurse's station. I wasn't in the clear way, but I heard shots down at the other nurse's station in that hall which was only about fifty feet or so. I jumped out in the middle of the hall, taking careful aim. Three shots went off really quick. Another one down. The guy I kicked was reaching for the automatic weapon of the other assailant that was shot. As soon as his hand hit the handle, I carefully took aim at him again and let her rip.

But at the other end of the hall, there was another man. He took careful aim at me. I put my foot on the wall and kicked off, kicking myself back into the nurse's station behind the counter. He let it rip. Down the hallway, bullets were flying everywhere. The nurse went to reach up to look out, but I grabbed her and jerked her down, putting my finger up against my lips.

Quietly, I waited there. As the assailant came down the hall pointing a machine gun at the nurse's station, waiting for me to poke my head out or someone so he could shoot them, I waited patiently as I slid down to the end. As soon as he got to the end of the hall, he pointed that gun at one end of the nurse's station and started shooting at the bottom trying to hit anybody that was ducked behind it, but before the bullets got to the nurse that was ducked down behind it, I slid a little farther out and let it rip. Five or six bullets went right into his torso.

I threw the gun down, walked down fifty feet to make sure there was no one else, walked around to the front, and then back out to the nurse's station where the doctor stood. I went back to the doctor and stood behind him. "Exit military mode," I said.

There were some local cops who were patrolling the area at the time. When they heard the gunshots, they quickly entered into the building, and there I stood behind the doctor as he looked at me. "What happened?"

The cops entered into the building one by one as others pulled up from them being called in. "Clear," one cop said.

"All clear here," another one said.

"Everyone okay?" the first one asked.

"Yes," the nurse said as she pointed at me. "That man saved our lives!"

I moved over behind the doctor. "How did you do that?" Dr. Dason said.

"How did I do what?" I had no idea what he was talking about.

He moved to the side and said, "How did you do that?" as he pointed at those men as the nurse began to explain to the cops what had happened.

The cop walked up to me." Alright, in your own words, tell us what happened."

"Well, I was standing here, and everything went black, and when I snapped out of it and got my sight back, Dr. Dason was standing right there in front of me. He had to be the one to do all this. He's a hero. Oh my God, he saved my life and the lives of all these people!"

The nurse stood there, shaking her head backward and forward. "That's not...," she started to say in a whisper, but Dr. Dason, seeing my puzzled look and confusion, his psychology kicked in really quick.

The cop looked at him and asked, "Is this so? Did you do this?"

"Why yes, it's so... I don't.... I don't know what came over me."

"Well, I can tell you one thing that came over you. Stupidity. This is a mafia kill gang, the underground terror. They would have killed everybody in this building had you not taken them down."

Dr. Dason looked at me. "Zon, you okay?" he asked.

I said, "I'm not sure. I'm a little confused."

He wrote down a number and an address. "Zon, I want you to meet me here. It's a friend of mine. At three o'clock tomorrow. Don't be late. It's important."

Now eager to get to the bottom of things, I couldn't wait until tomorrow, but I knew something was going on. The sense of danger had left as I walked out of the building, stepping over dead bodies. Confused and disoriented but still no fear. No remorse and no feeling for those that laid dead, but for some reason, I knew that this wasn't the underground terror.

I laid there that night on the couch where I was sleeping. I could hear voices out in the street where there was no one talking. I got up and went to the kitchen. The nurse, the man that I was now staying with, who was at the doctor's office, and also worked at the hospital with Dr. Dason, was sitting there at the table. "Zon, you're incredible," I heard him say, but his mouth didn't move.

I said, "What do you mean?"

He said, "Excuse me?"

I said, "What do you mean I'm incredible?"

His eyes got big. "I didn't say anything, Zon."

"Don't be funny. I heard you say that I was incredible. Now

what do you mean by it?"

"Zon, I didn't say anything. I was thinking that, and you are incredible. What you did today, it was spectacular, in a spooky kind of way."

"I don't know what you're talking about. Explain," I said.

"Zon, I was standing over in the next hall, perpendicular from the hall you were shooting down. I heard every word you said to the doctor, and now you can somehow know what I'm thinking because I haven't spoken anything until you spoke first."

"That's impossible. I heard you plain as day."

"I hear a lot of people plain as day," I stood there thinking to myself, "but sometimes their mouths don't move."

On the operating table, I believe, is when it happened. I went into cardiac arrest three times while the doctor operated on my head, removing the bone matter out of my brain. But it was the third time they brought me back.

The male nurse said, "It was at the operating table. Wasn't it?"

My eyes got big. "You knew what I was thinking?"

"Zon, you were white as a ghost. When electrical shock was introduced to you, it was like your veins swelled up to the top of your skin. Pure blue, and then they turned red, and then they disappeared back down into your flesh. Then, your heart got stable. Your vital signs got stable. Your brain activity was normal. That's when the doctor said, 'That's all I can do. Sew him up.'"

"I don't remember any of that," I told him.

He said, "Look, I've got a six o'clock shift. I've gotta go to bed."

"Good luck with that," I said as I laid back on the couch.

54

"And by the way, thanks for letting me stay."

"No problem. I know if I'm ever in trouble in the future, you'll be there for me."

"You can count on it," I said.

"Good night, Zon," he said as he left the room.

"Good night," I said as I laid back on the pillow.

Now I woke up early that next morning. It was a small apartment. The window shades weren't quite closed enough to keep the sun from penetrating through and shining right on my eyes. "Wow, that's bright," I thought as I got up off the couch.

After we had drank a cup of coffee and both got on our way, I spent a little time downtown, but that sense of danger came back over me about eleven o'clock. After remembering a few things here and there but not really being able to place them in my mind the right way, there was a car coming down the road, but it wasn't just any car. It was the way it was creeping down the road. I could feel them staring at me, whoever was in it. I didn't dare look.

I looked down at the piece of paper the doctor had given me the day before. "Elanoy and Fifth Avenue," I said as I looked at the sign. "Two thirty-three. Second floor, no doubt," I thought as I entered into the building. Suite 202.

As I opened the door, there was a big sliding glass window in a small room. There were no doors, just a window. There were four chairs, luxury chairs, nice and comfortable to sit in.

"Are you Zon?" she asked.

"Yes, ma'am, I am."

"Please have a seat. I'll let them know you're here."

"Them?" I asked. "Who's them?"

The doctors, of course, " she said as she closed the window.

After about three minutes, the door opened back up that I came in. There he stood. Dr. Dason. "How are you doing?" I asked him.

"Fine, Zon, come with me. I've got somebody I want you to meet."

"Dr. Dason, you're nervous for some reason."

"Yeah, I've been quite shaken up since yesterday. I apologize. I've never experienced anything even remotely close to that experience. That's what we need to talk about, Zon," he said as he led me down a hallway.

There was a room to the left. There were big fancy sofa couches, three of 'em to be exact. Leather chairs matching the couches and a big desk. Another doctor stepped out from around the desk with his hand held out. "Mr. Zon, I'm so glad to meet you. I'm Dr...." He gave me his name and told me his profession. He was head over the psychiatric department. "Zon, have you ever been in the military?" he asked.

"No, I don't think so, but I don't think I would remember if I had, being how I lost half of my brain."

"Yes, Dr. Dason has told me you were shot and lost your memory. He filled me in on what happened yesterday. It was amazing, but what is even more amazing is that you think Dr. Dason did all that military combat when in fact it was you. That's what I would like to talk to you about."

"Listen, Doc, I don't know what happened yesterday. Just like I told the cops, I was standing there one minute, and when I woke up, there were dead men everywhere. End of story."

"Have you had any other experiences like this?"

"No, none at all, oh... except for one. I could hear you talking when I came in, but your mouth wasn't moving."

He giggled a little bit and said, "Really, what was I saying?"

"Confounded pipe!"

When he heard this, he looked up and said, "Do what?"

I said, "That's what you were saying when I came into the room, without your mouth moving, confounded pipe."

He looked at Dr. Dason as he reached into his pocket and pulled out a broken pipe. "Dr. Dason, there is no way Zon could have known about this broken pipe. I had tucked it in my pocket as you two came in the door. Unless you told him about my broken pipe. Well, that's impossible because no one could have known what I was thinking, but that is exactly what I was thinking when you two walked in. Confounded pipe. Another broken one."

After a moment of silence, he said, "Zon, can you hear everybody without their mouth moving?"

"Only when they are upset about something, I think. You know, Doc, I ain't really sure. I just get these funny feelings when something is about to happen."

"Like yesterday? Do you remember the words, entering into military mode?"

"No, not really."

"That's what you said before you took down the assailants. Dr. Dason says it was almost robotical. He said you jumped off the walls, off the counters, and you took two of those assailants down like they were children with popguns, saving every life in the building."

"Look, Doc, I don't remember that. Like I told Dr. Dason and the cops, I thought Dr. Dason did all that. There was only one other male in the place, and he was much too feminine. No offense."

"None taken," Dr. Dason said. "He is a nurse."

I said, "Dr. Dason, look, I've got to get back to work. I've already taken half of a day off, and the best sales are in the afternoons."

"Zon, I'd like to talk to you again," the psychiatrist said. "Can you come back again?"

"I don't know. I'll think about it."

"Well, here's my card. Call me if you need anything and especially if you remember anything."

As I looked down to the card, I headed toward the door. I said, "Thanks but no thanks. Doc, I appreciate everything you've done for me, but it's time for me to go my way and get on with my life."

"Now wait a minute, Zon, You have some special gifts. Don't you want to share them with the world?"

"No, right now I just want to get on my feet and get my life together and try to figure out what went wrong. I appreciate everything you've done. I'll keep in touch."

"Do that, Zon. Please do that."

6

Now exiting the building, I got that sensation again. Someone was following me. As I walked down the sidewalk, a car pulled up beside me. I looked over. There were three men, one in the backseat and two in the front. The one on the passenger side yelled out a name. I ignored them as if they weren't talking to me.

"Hey you!" they yelled and yelled out the name again.

"You talking to me?" I asked.

"Oh, a wise guy, huh? Get over here." I walked over to the door.

"Ooh, you got a nasty bump on the head."

I said, "Yeah, I was shot."

"Yeah, I know. You remember who did it?"

The back window rolled down. "No, I don't remember who did it. I don't remember anything," I told them.

"So what are they calling you then?"

"They're calling me Zon. I'm working on getting my license and getting my social security number."

"So you don't remember anything, do you?" the guy in the backseat said. "Look Zon, get in. I want to talk you."

I looked around and said, "What the hell." I climbed in the backseat.

"Listen Zon," he continued, "that's not your name. You work for me. You got shot three weeks ago. Another mob gang put a contract out on you. I'm afraid it's curtains for you, son. There ain't nothing I can do for you."

"I can take care of myself."

"Yeah, I can see that. You got a bullet hole in the head, no memory, and not knowing what to do, you won't last a day out on the street."

"You're wrong. I'm a different person now."

"You may be a different person, but you still work for me."

"Yeah, what's that supposed to mean?"

"Well, I take care of my men, you know what I mean, especially my top three men. One being you. Look Zon, I've been following you around a couple of days. You're an easy target. It's just a matter of time."

"What do you suggest I do?"

"Well, you've done killed two assassins, and the last one almost killed you."

"Yeah, like I said, I don't remember that. Listen fellas, I'm getting a new name, and I don't remember my old life. And I certainly don't want to work for you. I sense that you're not a good person."

"Now, now, Zon."

"Oh, it's Zon now?"

"If you like. I'll call you anything you want me to, but just remember, you owe me. You're in debt to me. Fifty grand, and fifty G's don't come easy. You got that kind of money?"

"No, I don't."

"But you came to me. I didn't come to you, and I bailed you out. Fifty G's you remember that. You still work for me."

Now after I heard that, I was pricked to the bone. Not knowing why I owed fifty grand or where I would get it, I thought about it very carefully. "Okay, what do you want me to do?"

"Same thing you've been doing all along, taking out the bad guys."

I looked at all three of 'em. "Ya'll are the bad guys," I told them.

"Yeah, but there's worse than us, and that's who you'll be taking out."

"Look, I'm not taking out anybody."

"Oh, I'm not too sure about that."

"Like I said, I can take care of myself. I'll get your money. Fifty grand."

"Oh no, it WAS fifty grand. I'm afraid it's way more than that now. You see there's interest."

"I don't like where this is going. If you've got a point to make, you better make it. I'm leaving."

"Look, wise guy, maybe you forgot who you're talking to."

The guy in the front seat turned around, "Yeah, Zon, maybe

you forgot your old pals."

"And who are you?"

"You know me, Knuckles."

"I don't know no Knuckles."

"Well that's too bad because me and you are best friends. And where did you get that ridiculous name?"

I looked down and said, "I don't know. It was on the hat that had a bullet hole on it."

"So Zon, huh?"

"Yeah."

"You know that's the name brand of the hat that you took off of a rack as we entered into a building. Now me and you got separated, and the next thing I knew you were laying dead on the ground."

"Dead?"

"Yeah, your brains were all over the place. Zon, if I would have known you were going to live, I wouldn't have left you like that. But with the cops coming and seeing your head all like that, well, you know, I had to get away."

"Look, Knuckles, I'm sorry, I don't remember you. And if we were friends, that's all fine and dandy, but it's all changed now. I'm not the same person you think I am."

The guy in the backseat said, "Look Zon, you've got to understand. You're a big part of my operation. Now we're friends. That's why I lent you the money in the first place. It got you out of a big jam, but you said you would work for me from then on out. And as far as the fifty grand, I don't care about that. You've made more than that back in one job, but losing you to this memory loss.... Surely you can remember something."

"The only things I remember are my doctors and the nurse that I'm staying with."

"Oh yeah, about that nurse, I got bad news for you. Some assassins went into the building after you left. I'm afraid if he was there, you might not want to go back."

"Why didn't you do something?"

"Look Zon, my number one priority was you. We couldn't let you get out of our sight."

That's when another car pulled up right on the other side, leaving the car that Knuckles and the gang were in between us. A guy poked out his head with a machine gun, and the guy in the backseat did the same thing. The windows were up. They let it rip. Two full magazines. I ducked down beside the car, and before I could raise up, they spun off.

"Get back in!" the boss said.

I jumped back into the car as quick as I could. The windows had cracks all in them. "What?!?!?!" I was puzzled at first.

"Ha huh, bullet proof glass. Haven't you ever heard of it?"

"Yeah but...."

"But what? This ain't the first time you've been shot at."

I touched the wound on my head. "I ain't talking about that," he said. "After 'em, you guys!"

As they turned the corner down at the end of the block, the driver mashed the gas hard. They were getting away. As we made the turn at the end of the block, he barely saw him make another turn at the end of the next block as he went around the corner to the right. The boss in the backseat said, "Go on down to the next road."

"But Boss, he turned here."

"Do what I said!" he yelled. As they drove down to the next block, the boss said, "Turn right here!"

There they came, straight on. "There they are, Boss. How'd you know that?"

"I didn't."

"They're coming straight at us, Boss. What do I do?"

"Mash the gas and hold tight."

Now by the time the cars met up head on, we got up to fifty-five miles per hour. But the other car was going way faster, and everybody being buckled in and secure and airbags being in the front seat, here I was with no seat belt, no airbag, and bullet proof glass that was shattered from the machine guns that had shot at it. They got the back glass as they were pulling up and sprayed all down the side, and as they were leaving, they shot the front windshield.

Now with all them cracks in there and me being a healthy guy, when the cars collided, I left the back seat, going past the front seat, pushing Knuckles beside of me as I went right by him, right into the windshield. As my head and upper torso squeezed in between the dash and the windshield, the rest of my body followed, along with the weight of it. The whole windshield gave way.

Now the driver and the passenger of the would be shooters, they didn't have bullet proof glass, obviously, as they came flying through at the same time I came flying through. Somehow I went right by them. It was like it was slow motion. Both of their necks were completely snapped as they hit the windshield. They went by me as I went by them. Right through the car I went as the man in the backseat went by me. But with the seat belt in the front seat and the head rest being in front of him, when his head hit the headrest, his hand went faster than his head, moving the seat belt over in front of him that was in the front seat. When the head rest gave way, his head got hooked onto the seat belt as he went by me. It wasn't a pretty sight.

There I went, right through the back windshield. He stopped in the front seat. Head down. Face down. The rest of his body laid over the dash and one leg went out of the window. That seat belt jerked the life right out of him.

I skidded down the cement, and I closed my eyes and laid there. I could hear Knuckles saying, "He couldn't have possibly lived through that." They shook it off and got out of the car, unscathed by the injuries the others suffered. Knuckles pulled out his gun and shot a few holes into their dead bodies. So did the driver.

That's when I heard Knuckles say as he saw me sit up on the cement, "He's some kind of zombie. Nobody could have lived through that." But his mouth didn't move. But they all stood there, all three of 'em looking at me, puzzled as to why I wasn't dead. I sat there looking at the windshield I had just came through, wondering why I wasn't dead myself. Three times, I heard Knuckles say I was a zombie, the walking dead, the man that couldn't die. They all thought these things. I could hear them plain as day, but their mouths weren't moving.

"Look, Zon," the boss said. "You help me get these contracts off of us. Obviously, they're trying to kill us, too." That's when he gave me the address of a building. "Meet Knuckles here. We're gonna set a little trap."

"A trap?" I said.

"Yeah, we're gonna get to the bottom of this. I don't like being shot at."

"What's this building got to do with setting a trap?"

"Well, it ain't this building. It's the one it attaches to. I'll explain it all to you. Meet me on the fourth floor," Knuckles said. "We've been planning this for a while. If you had your memory, you would know that."

"Yeah, why is that?"

He said, "It's easy, Zon." He laughed a little bit. "I don't know if I can get used to that new name, but it sounds pretty cool anyway," as he thought to himself, "Zon Zombie," but he finished the sentence with, "it was your idea."

Now puzzled at what I heard, I know I must have not been a good person, but yet here I am, a new person, a new way of thinking. I had no idea, but it was starting to make sense. Four dead in the doctor's office the day before. Three laid dead in the streets today.

That's when we all split up. No doubt the cops would be there soon. I had to check on my friend. But upon arriving at the apartment, there was a bullet hole in the door right where the lock was so I pushed on the door. It opened up.

Nothing at first. Wondering if my friend got out before or after, I entered into the room slowly at first, but looking over where I had slept on the couch the night before, I didn't see anything at first. But there it stuck out beside the coffee table behind the couch, a white sock and a shoe with a foot in it. I knew those shoes anywhere, special order, male nurse shoes.

I walked around the other end, and there he laid. Assassinated. Russian style. Two bullets in the back of the head. My heart was thumping really hard by now, but not for fear and not for love of my dear friend who was the first one that I met when I woke up with no memory, like a brother, a mother, a sister, maybe even a father, I don't know, but the anger filled me from head to toe. My blood was boiling. I felt hot as if I were in a fire, but I still sensed danger.

I knew he was in the bedroom, and I knew death waited for me. But I didn't care. I picked up the coffee table with the lamp on it, and as the lamp and stuff fell out from the coffee table, I took the legs and I kicked that bedroom door open as I held the coffee table in front of me. Toomp toomp toomp, the wood flew from the coffee table right into my chest. I ran straight toward the assailant, the would be killer and the murderer of my friend. With one side of the coffee table legs pointing right at him, I ran straight into his chest.

Toomp toomp, I backed away to see the damage that I had done. There he was propped up against the nightstand with the legs going through his chest. His knees hit the floor. The legs wouldn't let him fall any farther as he knelt there, his head rolled back

I was panting for air when I looked down at my chest and stomach. Five holes. Wood splinters poking out from my chest. Road rash from skidding. I was a mess. A broken arm, broken hand, a broken foot. I looked terrible.

I went to the bathroom, turned on the hot water, and pulled the shower thing to make the shower run as I stepped into it. After pulling the wood splinters anywhere from one inch to four inches out of my chest and stomach, the water washed the blood down into the tub.

But something unusual was happening. I felt the wound, the first one on my stomach. There was a lump there, but I didn't feel the pain. I reached in with my finger and my thumb, puzzled that I was able to do it. I could touch the bullet, and when I did, I pulled it out. It was flat on one end, mushroomed around. I looked down at the other wound and did the same thing.

I tried to do it in my chest, but the bone was in the way. But I looked in the cabinet. There was a pair of chemo-stats. I pushed them deep into the cavity of my chest. I was able to get two more bullets out. But the other one I couldn't find, and it being close to my heart, I was afraid to dig any deeper.

When I looked down at the first wound, it was all fizzy and white, and with the water rushing from the shower head, I stepped in front of it again. It was just a scar. As I took off the wringing wet clothes and left them there, I quickly hunted for some more to slip on. After I did, I left the place, not having any place to go.

That's when Dr. Dason got a phone call. "Hello."

"It's me," I said

"Zon, how are you doing?"

"I'm not doing too good. I got shot again."

"I'll meet you at the hospital."

"No need for that, Doc. I need a place to stay tonight. My

wounds are okay."

He gave me his address and told me to come right over. Upon entering into his house, he said, "Zon, I'm glad to see you. I thought you were shot."

"I was." I lifted up my shirt.

"Those scars weren't there yesterday," the doctor said.

"I know, right?"

"What happened?" he asked.

"Doc, I don't know what's happening. It's been the craziest day. I was shot. I went through a car window, skidded down the road. I got shot five times. This was the road rash."

"It's just smooth skin, Zon."

"I know. That's what I've been trying to tell you."

"It's just a little scarred looking from the past."

"But it wasn't like that yesterday. An hour ago, I was shot five times in the chest and stomach, but now there are nothing but scars."

"Come with me. I'm taking you down to the emergency room. If you've been shot, there will be bullets in there. If they healed over that fast, you will still need to get them out."

"I done got 'em out, all except for the one over my heart."

"Let me take you to the hospital and get an x-ray. If it's that close to your heart, it's gonna have to come out."

"It ain't there no more."

"What do you mean it ain't there no more?"

"It's dropped down to my stomach. I can feel it."

"Now Zon, you know that's impossible."

"Look I need a place to stay tonight. I'm not going to no

hospital."

"Sure, I've got a spare bedroom," he said.

Exhausted with no place to stay and no place to go, I assured the doctor that I was okay. It was right before the sun rose when I heard a thump. It woke me up, but it wasn't close to me. The doctor's house was really nice. It had an upstairs, four or five bedrooms, six rooms downstairs. He had done fairly well for himself. But I killed him. As soon as I made that phone call earlier the night before, I marked him as a dead man, and when I heard that thump, I knew that to be so.

I knew I was a bad man, and I had done some bad things. Before a moment, everything went black, and then my eyesight came back as I stood there. "Not again," I thought to myself. "Did I just black out like I did at the doctor's office?"

I stepped out into the hall. It was a mess. Table were turned over. Chairs were turned over. Lamps were busted, and the doorway to the doc's bedroom, but it was only minutes before as I had stood in the guest room and heard the thump of a dead body falling to the floor when I said, "Militant mode activated."

Opening up the bedroom door, there he had stood, a six inch silencer on an automatic pistol. Before he could even touch the trigger, I grabbed the silencer with my right hand as he pulled the trigger back. Fifteen shots went off as he took his left hand with his fingers straight out aiming toward my throat. I moved to the side as his hand went right by my neck. As his arm went past my neck, I had already raised my elbow up into his chin, still holding onto the gun as I felt the warmth of the silencer as the bullets finished firing and ran out of the gun.

The hit man let go of the gun with his right hand. As I pinned him up against the wall by his neck with my elbow, he punched me in the midsection and then kicked me over to the other side of the hall. That was the first table. As I came off the wall with my foot, I grabbed the table, jerking everything off onto the floor as I slung it to his head. He ducked, kicked off the bottom of the wall underneath the table, and pushed off the other wall back toward me as I went by him. He kicked for my midsection at the same time I kicked toward his, kicking us both back toward the wall of the hallway.

By this time, we were halfway down the hall toward the bedroom. A karate chop here. A counter karate chop there. A kick here. A kick there. Flipping over each other and then back again. We ended up in the bedroom where the doc laid face down.

This guy was really fast. Back on our feet we stood. He blocked every hit as I blocked every hit that he would have made. As fast as lightning I thought he was, but I didn't tire as my fists kept hitting toward him. I would block one. He would block one. I would block another one. He would block another one. Just as fast as we could go. But I didn't tire.

He had held his breath during this whole period of standing there trying to get a punch in. Then he had to take a breath. When he did, he came around with the left hand and I blocked it. Then he came around with the right hand, and I blocked it. But this time, I pulled both of my arms in as he took a breath. I took my fist as fast and as hard as I could. Straight punch. Right into his chest. He fell back, tripping over the dead body of my good friend, the doctor.

He came out from behind his back with an eight inch blade. Kicking his feet up and then back underneath him, he quickly raised back up on his feet, lounging over the body, but I stood there calm, cool, and collected. And there he stopped right in front of me, face to face, looking at me as I looked back at him.

That's when he faded and slumbered down with the knife sticking out from underneath his rib cage, right dead center of his chest. I stood there for a moment over his dead body, watching the blood ooze out. I walked back to the guest room where the doctor was so kind to let me stay the night at and stood in the exact same place I had started from. "Exit military mode," I said.

Now I walked out of the bedroom after carefully examining what happened and still knowing nothing. I quickly left the doctor's house. With dead bodies everywhere, there were going to be questions asked, but I wasn't going to be the one they asked, I thought quickly as I left. On my way out, I grabbed the doctor's keys and thought I would borrow his ride especially since he didn't need it any longer. I carefully locked the house as I left.

7

Now, I was driving downtown as I usually did, obviously because I remember some of the buildings. Now why was it? Some things I could remember plainly, and other things I couldn't remember at all. Something was protecting me.

I was drawn to a bar. The neon signs flashed in my mind as I passed by. I couldn't stand it, so I stopped. Now calm, cool, and collected, I walked over and sat down at the bar. I hadn't noticed, but there was a gentleman sitting beside me. He tilted up his hat as his eyes came out from underneath the brim. "That's funny," he said with a deep scary voice. "I thought you couldn't remember."

It was Knuckles. I said, "Remember what?"

"Well you must remember something. You and me have been coming here for years."

"Look, Knuckles, I don't know nothing. If I could remember, I would say so."

He said, "Yeah, but you must remember something."

"Yeah, the neon lights kept flashing in my eyes deep in the back of my mind."

"Look, I gotta go do a job tonight," he said.

"Yeah, so I've been told. I meet you at a building, so and so address. We do such and such thing. I understand all that."

"No, you don't understand. That's above what we usually do. Me and you, we're balancers."

"Balancers?" I said.

"Yeah, we balance out the organized crime, you and me."

"How's that?"

"Well, the bosses loan people money. We go collect it. Bad drug deals, bad money deals, bad gun deals. We make it even. That's why we're called balancers."

"Sounds more like a bar bouncer? Did you come up with all this stuff?"

"Huh, huh, huh," he giggled a little with his deep raspy voice. "No, you did. You've been feeding me this crap for years."

"Oh, now it's crap," I said as he used a few choice other words.

"Yeah, it ain't worth a crap if you ain't my partner," he said with a few choice words added in. "So what's it gonna be?"

"Alright, what do I do?"

"That's the spirit," he said.

I left the doctor's car at the bar with the keys in the ignition. The worse thing that could happen is that somebody would steal my car. Oh, but it wasn't mine. As I climbed into his car,

Knuckles took me uptown. It was the black section, and there was a black mob boss in the section But I didn't know what was going on. Knuckles filled me in. He said, "I had to call and get permission."

"Permission to do what?" I asked.

"To come on this turf."

As we pulled up to a building, there were black guys all over the place. Some looked meaner than others. A tall black guy walked up to me. I obviously looked like I was in control. Knuckles looked tough enough alright, but when it came to smarts, well, he was dumb as skunk water. I didn't know it, but I had always told him every step to take. But this time, I didn't know exactly what to do, but my instincts kicked in.

"What you white boys doin' over here?"

I said, "Back up. We got permission from your boss." As I put my hands on his chest and walked on by him, they knew I meant business.

Two stories up, we stepped off the elevator. Third floor. Second door to the right. We stood in front of it. Knuckles said, "This is the place. He paid off the black mob boss to hide in this area."

But it was what the black guy said as I walked on past. He was talking to another guy. He said, "What do I care if them white guys kill each other?" But were we there to kill?

Knuckles knocked on the door. Tap, Tap. Then paused, then tap, tap, and quickly moved to the side as I obviously had instructed him to do in the past. There was no answer. Knuckles reached over and banged on the door again, only louder this time.

"I know you're in there," he said. "You've hid long enough."

Shots went off. Knuckles had just moved his fist from the door when the wood splinters started spraying off the door across the hallway along with bullets. After shooting for a moment, the firing stopped.

Knuckles stepped back and kicked in the door. When the door opened, I was to the side of it, but I could see in plainly. He was small in stature, but he had that gun pointing straight at me as he dove across the room.

Now earlier on before we got there, Knuckles had asked me if I had a gun. I said no. He reached under the seat and pulled out a .357. Now it was a big ol' gun. It had a nine inch barrel on it. I said, "You got many of these, do you?"

He said, "No, I don't have none of those. That's actually your gun."

"So I use a cannon, do I?"

"Yeah, among other guns you carry on you."

Now as I stood there with the hammer pulled back on my .357, I could somewhat remember the bullets. Someone was loading bullets for me.

"Oh yeah," whoever it was said, "when you use these bullets, it's gonna pack a wallop, and it's going to kick quite a bit, heavier grain bullet and this soft lead, well you don't need hollow points." But who was talking? Who was making the bullets? I couldn't remember.

I let it rip, just one shot. It hit him in the kneecap. It almost blew his knee right off. He would never use that knee again. That's if he lived at all.

"Please!" he said. "Don't kill me! Please, oh God, don't kill me! It hurts so bad!" he said as we walked into the room.

There was a black girl putting her head out of the apartment door next to him and a few others down the hall as they watched us enter into the room. I shut the door.

Knuckles said, "You owe the boss two hundred grand."

"Listen, it's the interest. I only borrowed eighty."

"Yeah, but you're past the deadline, and you know the rules. If you pass the deadline, you gotta pay extra."

"But I was already paying one hundred and sixty thousand."

Now when Knuckles was going to kill somebody, he liked to use a knife, and his reputation was ten minutes. He could make a person feel the most pain before they had a heart attack and went into cardiac arrest. Of course, after that, they died, and it was obvious as he pulled out a big old knife what he was fixing to do.

I cocked that hammer back on that .357 and pointed it at his head as I told Knuckles, "I'm just gonna kill him."

"No, wait a minute. I got the money. At least what I owed him from the start. The other forty grand I can get. Please don't kill me."

"Okay, I won't kill you," I said. "Where's the money?"

He looked over at the coffee table. I didn't see anything at first, but right underneath the coffee table, I noticed it was boxed in. He said, "I can get it. It's real close."

But I could hear him plain as day even though his mouth wasn't moving. "The money's boxed into the coffee table."

Knuckles rammed a knife right into his chest, and he started to cut downward. His eyes got big as he pointed over at the coffee table. But it was too late. Knuckles cut all the way down to his belly. He didn't make a sound.

Now earlier on, this guy was a small time crook. But little did I know that Knuckles had it in for him. It was only three weeks earlier when the little mouse paid Knuckles' cousin a visit. She was a teenage girl, seventeen. She was also a prostitute, passing herself off as twenty-five. She had lured him with her love. Of course, just to get money. But after bedding him, he refused to pay, and the one thing he hated to be called was worthless. He had killed his mother, and his dad trying to protect her, he killed him, too. After years of being called worthless, he had had enough, and now his would be lover was calling him worthless.

"Pay me what you owe me, you worthless mouse."

He smacked her across the jaw, busting her eardrum.

"You know you ain't gonna get by with that," she told him

"Yeah, who's gonna stop me?"

"When my cousin hears about this, you'll know who's gonna stop you."

That's when he took out a knife and stabbed her in the stomach. "No," she said as he grabbed her by the back of the neck with the other hand.

"I'm afraid I won't have no further use for you now," he said as he ripped the knife upward.

And now he laid there dying, thinking on what he had done. But it was a local hooker who told Knuckles about it, and he took it on his own to collect the money when he found out where he was.

I went over to the coffee table. There was no door on the sides or the front or the back. I tapped on the bottom. It was thin, thin enough to let me know there was something in there. But I couldn't figure it out.

Knuckles said, "Why don't you see if it lifts up? Take that lamp off the top."

I grabbed the side of it and lifted the whole thing up. It went over to the side. The lamp and everything went onto the floor. It was only hours earlier that he had went to another mob boss and borrowed two hundred and seventy thousand dollars, and there it laid, wrapped up in a circle. Twelve big rolls of money.

"Two hundred of it goes to the boss, but we get half of it. There's fifty for you and fifty for me," Knuckles said.

"What about the other seventy grand?"

"Well, it's thirty-five for you and thirty-five for me."

After leaving, as we walked back to the car, the same black guy said, "You just done us a favor. That's all. I would've killed him myself."

Ignoring his every word, Knuckles got in and cranked the car up. I got in on the other side. I said, "I don't think we're out of trouble yet."

He said, "No, we still gotta get out of this neighborhood without getting killed. The Asians won't like it."

The mob bosses have been feuding about territory ever since there was a mob. There was a leader of the black section. At one time, there was even a Jewish mob. They got completely wiped out, along with a whole bunch of others. Now it was just down to a handful. Waiting to be shot at and not knowing if we were going to make it out or not, we finally made our way back to the bar. As

I got out of the car, Knuckles said, "I'll see you tonight."

I knew what he was talking about, the building, the address. I looked down at Knuckles' pants. I said, "You might wanna change your pants."

"Yeah, I usually do after a job. No big deal," he said, looking down at the blood.

"I guess I'll see you later," I said.

All along, I was remembering more. There were many jobs, but where did I put the money? Here I was with eighty-five thousand and not knowing where to hide it. But I kept remembering the old buildings, and one building in particular stood out among them all. I remembered the stairwell, the broken elevator, the leaky roof that leaked down through the stairwell, and its big open walkway that went around the top of the first floor. It was a good forty feet high and thirty feet off the floor. It had an open walkway all around the inside wall, and the first set of steps in the stairwell went straight up to that floor. I kept remembering things about the building as I made my way up to the roof. "There's nothing here," I thought to myself.

There was an old air conditioner. They call 'em water coolers. But what significance did it have? Why did I remember it so clear? I walked around the big air conditioner. Then I saw a manhole with a handle on it, and through the handle was a piece of pipe shoved down into a hole into the floor back behind the door. By the looks of it, you would think it would never open, and you probably wouldn't have even tried by the rust that was on the handle of the door. But I had to take a look.

Now that old cooler had been leaking for years and the roof

was kinda spongy as I walked across two inches of water, but when I moved that handle downward, the door popped open after I removed the piece of steel that was blocking the handle from moving. It was dark at first. But after my eyes focused for a moment, I looked around. There was nothing.

But when I tried to pull my head back out of the door, my head hit a box that was over the door. It was a wooden box. It was about nine inches tall, about a foot and a half wide, and two feet long. It sat on two rails over the door. After I rubbed my head a moment or two with a few choice words, I lifted the box up. It was quite heavy, but when I let it down, it was full of money. A little black bag that had diamonds in it, but why could I remember certain things? But I couldn't remember my name? The doctor said I would never regain my memory, but here I am remembering things.

I'm rich. There must be over a million dollars worth of money here, a few gold bars. They were little bitty bars of gold, but there was a significant amount, at least three hundred thousand dollars worth which made the box quite heavy. I thought to myself, "I need a new location." Judging from the roof and the sponginess under my feet, the building was old. Just like many buildings I had seen the tops of, some of them were burnt, and you could tell somebody had lit fires on them. I had a thing for old buildings. I just couldn't see historical benefactors being torn down, or burnt, or destroyed.

Then I had another memory of gangs beating me up, but the buildings seemed to come to life and protect me somehow. I've been shot at and missed. But the gun was two feet away, pointing at my chest. Impossible as it may sound, I have ventured through life unscathed and unharmed. But then I took my hand and felt of the scar on my head. I thought, "Why did this one hurt me? What was so different? Was it the buildings? Who shot me and why? But the time I got shot, Knuckles was with me."

I met him at the address that night. I had questions. I wanted answers. We met in the front of the building. He said, "Follow me." We walked down an alley behind the building. We headed up the steps to a door. It was a steel door.

I said, "Wait a minute, Knuckles. What happened?"

"What do you mean what happened?"

I pointed at my head. "Tell me exactly what happened."

"Zon, it was an accident," he said. "I give you my word it was an accident."

"Go on. Finish the story."

"We had done a job like usual."

"You mean, like usual, we killed somebody."

"Well, yeah, that's what we do," he said. "Only this time, we were followed. It was just a bad thing, that's all. You got out on the passenger side. It was an old black van. Zon, there's no way I could have known it was you. You went around the van before I even knew what you were doing. The driver got on in." He pulled open his shirt and showed me a bullet wound. "He shot me right here. In the back of the van, I heard another shot. That's when I was able to shoot the driver. Another guy stepped out from the back of the van with a machine gun. I shot him, too. Now Zon, don't get mad. I saw the shadow of another man coming out from the back of the van on the ground...."

"That was me, no doubt."

"I'm sorry."

"So you shot me in the head?!?! Knuckles, you shot me in the head?!?!"

He hung his head down to the ground, shaking his head backward and forward. "It was an accident." Now Knuckles, looking down, was thinking how sorry he really was as he spoke it with his lips.

Now Knuckles wasn't very smart. But that didn't explain why that gun shot wound messed me up so bad. I've been shot with machine guns, stabbed, cut, hung, thrown off of buildings, been blown up in buildings, fires. I was remembering more and more, but why did this penetrate my head?

Knuckles was almost afraid, almost. "Zon, you're not gonna kill me for this, are you? We've been best friends. We've been only friends. You know I'd never hurt you. But when I saw half of your head gone, and you didn't breathe, I just figured you were dead. I'd have never left you there, had I known."

"What do you mean, you left me there?"

"I left you at the hospital," he said.

"So you're the one that took me to the emergency room?"

"Yeah, of course."

"How long was I at the hospital?"

"I don't know, Boss. You was there a long time."

"Boss? Why'd you call me boss?"

"Well, you've always been over me, Zon. You've been my boss since the first day I started. You remember that. A dirty cop. He had it in for you. I took him out. I've taken out a couple of dirty cops, a dirty judge, a dirty D.A. Everybody's gotta pay when they don't pay, you know what I mean."

"Yeah, I know what you mean, Knuckles."

I grabbed the handle to the door and opened it up. I turned back and said, "Look, don't shoot me in the head again."

"Oh, that won't happen again."

"Good, make sure it don't."

He said, "I've got some bad news. This time they're expecting us."

"What? You mean we're walking into a trap?"

"I'm afraid so."

"Maybe you oughta let me in on this plan, Knuckles," I sighed.

He took an oozy out from underneath his jacket and put it in my hand. He took another nine millimeter that was automatic and put it in my other hand as he said, "The boss wants us to spray this building down, killing everybody and anything that moves. This is Big B's place. Them two guys out in the front are some of his hounds. He's got about ten of 'em in the building."

"Yeah, where's he at?"

"I don't know. He's somewhere in the building. If we kill everybody, we'll make sure we get him." Then he screwed in the silencer on his nine millimeter on his automatic. Then he screwed in the silencer on the oozy and then handed me two silencers to do the same thing.

I said, "What, no silencer for my .357?"

"Well, Boss, would a silencer even work on that thing?"

"Probably not," I said. Knuckles had given me a shoulder

strap where I put the .357. The oozy hung on a piece of leather beside it on the other side.

Now after walking down the hallway a little ways, I had remembered another thing about Knuckles. He loved to blow up things. Now here we stood again, facing death. That's when he pulled out a hand grenade and threw it down to the end of the hall.

After the ringing, I held up the gun with the silencer on it. I said, "Knuckles what good are the silencers if you're gonna throw grenades?"

"I don't know, Boss. I just don't like the loud sound," he answered as if it made sense.

I held my hand open toward the part he had just blown up. "And that ain't a loud sound?"

"Yeah, I guess it is," he said, holding his ear on the left side as his ears were ringing as he walked past me.

Here came three of 'em. One on one side of the hall, one on the other one, and one in the middle. The lights were blown out. The building was damaged. I told Knuckles, "Don't destroy the building. They're historical landmarks. They've been here over a hundred years."

"But the boss said...."

"I don't care what the boss said. Do not destroy the building," I demanded.

8

Now it's been years. One job after another one, and they've accepted the name Zon Zombie. Everybody has. Switching from one mob boss to another one. After switching my money from building to building and hiding it carefully, I was running low on cash one day. Now on some buildings, they had fire hoses that were on a reel. You would grab the fire hose, pull it out, turn the water on, put the fire out, roll the reel back up, and turn the water off, but this particular fire hydrant was on the wall. You could slide it out. It's kinda hard to explain, but that's where I hid my money, back behind the fire hose or the fire station, whatever you call it. If you opened up the door, you wouldn't see it, but if you grabbed a hold of the door's edge and pulled gently, the whole case would come out of the wall like another door.

I thought nobody knew this but me, but being out of cash and all, I made my way to the fire hydrant where I had stashed the cash along with the other gold and diamonds. I was up over two million dollars. A little here, a little there, but when I reached for the box after opening up the hole way, there was nothing. No box, no money, no gold, no diamonds. All my stuff was gone.

I closed it back up and scratched my head. I walked down the steps, out the building, and down the steps, out the front door. It was the next building across the street. A young teenager stood there looking at me. My senses kicked in as he disappeared inside of the building.

I casually walked across the road and walked into the building. He disappeared at the top of the steps. Casually but briskly, I walked toward him as I walked up the steps. As I reached the top of the steps and looked down the hallway, he disappeared into an apartment. There was an A side and a B side. It was A216. I stood there, looking at the numbers.

I heard the teenagers inside cursing and ranting and raving. "I'm gonna be the biggest gangster in this city," one of 'em said as I stood there listening through the door. "Yeah, I'm gonna buy me the biggest gun. When I shoot somebody, they're gonna die from the fear of it."

Standing there in amazement of what I was hearing, I couldn't believe it. They had all that money, and still all they could think of was organized crime, murder, rape, killing. With over two million dollars at their disposal.

I kicked the door in hard as I could. I aimed at their heads, each one of 'em, one at a time, and right before I shot 'em, I moved the gun to the right where the bullets flew by each one of 'em's heads. There were three of 'em.

One fell back to the couch. The other fell back to the chair, and the third one fell onto the floor, scooting backward as he did. I walked up to him, the one on the floor, and aimed at his belly with that big old .357, and right before I fired, I moved it over to the side where it shot into the floor. By this time, the other two were screaming, "No! Please!"

I pointed the gun at the other one in the chair, aimed the gun at his belly, and did the same thing, shooting at the chair. Then I did the same thing to the one on the couch. They were screaming in horror as I stood there one after another one, clicking the gun. There were no more shots, but this time I was pointing the gun at each one of 'em while I was clicking it.

The boy on the floor, he messed himself and passed right out. I thought he had a heart attack. The other two were shaking in terror. "Steal from me, will ya?" I said.

The boy on the couch, about nineteen, said, "Mister, we didn't steal it. We just found it. That's all."

"Well, you found the wrong stash this time."

"Here, here's your box. It's all there."

The boy on the floor woke up and raised up a little bit. "Are you gonna kill us?"

"I've decided to let you live on one condition. You go back to school and get out of crime," I pointed that .357 at 'em again, each one of 'em, "or else, the next time I come calling will be the last time. And if you find my stash again, well, you better hope you don't." When I looked down, their pants were wet, all three of 'em.

I saw one of the boys years later. He was the manager of an ice cream parlor for a while, and then he became the owner of it. I heard of his incident where local gangs would come and collect money from him for their protection. That's when I put in the word, Zon Zombie's protecting him. No more gangs came around. To collect money, that is. If they weren't buying, they weren't staying. I don't know what happened to the other two boys, but it looked like this one made up his mind to do what was right.

I never let him know that I was protecting him. But after a while, word got out on the street, and it finally got back to the boy. He remembered all that I had done, and one day, he saw me on the sidewalk. "Mr. Zombie," he said, "you remember me?" He paused for a moment and then said, "I just want to thank you."

I asked for what as if I didn't know. "Well, for two or three things, matter of fact," he answered. "One, for the protection and not charging me for it. The other, for not killing me. And the other, for teaching me such a valuable lesson. That living and having a life were two totally different things. Mr Zombie, I'm married now, and I've got two kids, thanks to you. I ain't making a killing, but I do own my own place of business."

I pulled out a roll of money. I often rolled up twenty or thirty thousand and would stick it in my pocket for spending money. I put it in his hand. "Spend this on your wife and kids. Maybe business will pick up for you. Who knows?"

And it did. I might have helped with that a little bit. It wasn't long before he had a chain of restaurants and was able to retire on a modest one hundred thousand a year. That was the last time I saw him. But I always got good reports.

I got reports of the other two boys. One was in the big house, death row, manslaughter. The other one went crazy. They put him in the insane asylum. His wife left him after his youngest kid died. He was no good. Neither was his wife. They were just pill heads. But after his wife took his last son away and left him, not knowing where they were or how to get a hold of 'em, it drove him crazy. The last I heard, he was still there.

Now like I said, it had been years, many jobs with Knuckles. He asked me one day, "Boss, how do you do that?"

"How do I do what?"

"That military mode stuff."

"Knuckles, what are you talking about?"

"Like that last building we were in. You stood there and said military mode activate. And then you started bouncing off the walls, killing people left and right. I've never seen nothing like it."

"Knuckles, you've been watching too many movies."

"Listen, Zon, I saw it with my own eyes, several times. When you're through, you say, exit military mode, and act like nothing ever happened."

I felt of my head. It was that damn doctor. What did he do to me? "How many times has this happened?" I asked Knuckles

"Four that I've seen with my own eyes. Like when we went into the restaurant. Three machine gunners, you dodged the bullets, took 'em out."

I remembered the restaurant. We went there to take out one of the mob bosses. We would take out one, and another would rise in his place. Organized crime was a big business. But the one that we were against, the underground terror, were the rapers and the murderers for no reason, like wild bikers, not having an agenda, waiting for death in every situation. Kill and be killed. We weren't like that. The boss I usually worked with was very organized, but now he had a hit on his life and so did I.

It was a bad deal. Guns were to be sold and managed by us. But when we went to collect the money, another mob boss found out about the deal and sent some guys over. It was a big shootout. They took the money and the guns. Well, the ones we were selling the guns to blamed it on us and put a contract out on us. Let's just say it didn't end well for them, but I had blacked out. According to Knuckles, I had taken 'em all out, but I couldn't remember nothing about it.

Now, we were high up on another building, another deal going bad. Knuckles was down in the car. It was drugs. They would drop off the drugs. I would pick 'em up. Of course, leaving money with 'em, but this time, there were six of them. A simple pickup. A simple drop off, and back down to the car I would go.

Only this time, the drug cartels were no longer going to use this particular boss to smuggle in their drugs with, and with this being their last batch and obviously their last money, they picked me up, all six of 'em, and they threw me off the building. And then they walked away.

Now when they came out of the building, there I was sitting in the car. Knuckles got out, pointing a machine gun at all six of 'em. That's when I lowered down the window and looked out. When they saw me, they turned white as ghosts. Knuckles opened fire, shooting all six of them. He went over and grabbed the drugs and the money, then got back into the car, and we drove off.

But just moments before they went into the stairway, the railing that goes down beside the fire escape, that thick piece of steel caught my foot, and as I went down, the rail ripped away from the side of the steps, letting me all the way down to the ground. Nice and easy like. And as soon as my back touched the ground, the rail let go, and with my own eyes, I watched it go back up onto the railing of the steps.

"Did that just happen?" I wondered to myself. I knew it wasn't the first time the buildings had helped me. But what happened to military mode? How did they get the drop on me? There were a lot of things I couldn't add up and I couldn't explain, and with things not adding up, the pieces to the puzzle just didn't fit. It was time to get checked out, but who could I trust? Nobody.

I said, "Knuckles, we've got to get to the bottom of this. I've gotta find out what that doctor did to my head. The headaches are getting worse."

We walked into the emergency room, and on the floor where surgeries are performed, we made it to the locked doors. Not being able to get through the locked doors, I stood there a minute. A nurse came around with a badge. She said, "Can I help you gentleman? This area is off limits. All guests have to go to the next floor down and get a visitor's pass, and even then, you are not supposed to be on this floor."

I said, "Okay, well, we'll just make our way down to the next floor."

She held up her pass in front of this little box at the doors. One opened one way. The other opened the other way. She walked through them. I turned around and walked through them with her. She turned around again and said, "Look....."

Before she could say another word, Knuckles opened up his jacket, the side the oozy was on, and then her haughty spirit humbled down quickly. "What are ya'll gonna do?" she asked.

"You just keep walking," Knuckles told her.

Then we went through some swinging doors, surgery. "That's good," the doctor said. "Nurse, stitch him up. We're finished."

Everybody looked up at us, and one said, "Sir you'll have to leave. You aren't supposed to be in here."

That's when I pulled out my .357. I said, "There ain't nobody going nowhere."

I pointed at the doctor that had just done the surgery. I said, "If you're finished with him, I've got a little job for you. Knuckles, you make sure nobody leaves this room."

The surgeon stepped away from the patient that was on the bed and walked over toward me. I swayed the gun toward the door as he walked through down to x-ray. "What do you need?" he asked nervously.

"You see this scar on my head?" I said. "I need you to x-ray and tell me what it is."

"How did you get the scar?"

"I was shot," I said as we walked down to the x-ray room.

When we got there, there was a young nurse there. The doctor said, "We need an x-ray of his head. Make haste and get it ready quickly."

After a few minutes, he got an x-ray, and then I walked them back to his office. He put the x-rays up on a big light on a panel.

He said, "That's odd."

"What is it, Doc?" I asked. I clicked the hammer back.

He quickly said, "That won't be necessary."

"I'll tell you what's necessary. You just tell me what I need to know. Now what the hell is it?"

He said, "I honestly don't know. You see this right here, it's your cerebral cortex. This is your frontal lobe, and this is your visual cortex. This little square thing here looks like some kind of chip or something. It has fiber optics coming off of it, hooking to your frontal lobe and your cerebral cortex. These here," he said as he pointed to the screen on the x-ray, "are fiber optics going to your visual cortex."

"What does all that mean?"

"Somebody's been tampering with your brain," he said.

"Is that even possible?"

He said, "No, we don't have this technology in this day and time. It must be some kind of military stuff."

That's when I thought quickly. Military mode. I've heard several people say that I said that, but why can't I remember? But with the surgeon that did this dead, my good friend the doctor, who was so conveniently my friend after the surgery.... I now know he had a different agenda, but what and why?

It was so long ago. I'm sure his house and all of his records are gone by now. Then I got to thinking about the psychiatrist he sent me too, his good friend, he said. "Yeah, good for what?" I thought to myself.

"Knuckles, take me to this address. We're gonna pay this guy a visit."

After leaving the hospital in an uproar, we quickly went uptown. It was going on five o'clock. He was about to leave his office as I opened up the door. "Ah, just the man I wanna talk to," I said

"What?!? Who are you, and what do you want? I'm closing now. I have to go home."

"You don't remember me, do you?"

"No, why would I? What do you want with me? You're not one of my patients."

"Oh, but on the contrary, I am one of your patients. You remember, Mr. Confounded Pipe."

His eyes got big. He was puzzled and startled. He thought back to how his doctor friend had gotten murdered along with others. He was questioned, but he knew nothing. But now I had questions for him, and I knew he knew something.

"I'm only going to ask you this once. If you lie to me, it won't be good for you."

"Listen, Mister."

"Mister Zombie to you."

"Well, that fits. So that's the name you chose for yourself?"

"I won't get into all that, but this is another thing," I said, pointing to my head.

"Listen, Mister Zombie, or Zon," he said, trying to play friendly now. "I had nothing to do with that. I was just a psychiatrist that was supposed to follow up."

"Follow up. What do you mean?"

"Well, the military chose you."

"What are you talking about?"

95

"They were keeping track of you. You had been beaten up, stabbed, shot. Most of theses were fatal wounds, but you lived. When you came in with a gun shot to your head, it was the militant part of the CIA. The generals and all got together..."

"Why haven't they been in my life for years?"

"I don't know, Mr. Zombie. Honest, I don't know anything."

That's when I pulled out my .357 and pulled back the hammer with it pressed against his forehead. "That just ain't good enough. What did they do to me?"

"It's just a little chip, that's all. Something went wrong with the remote of it."

"Why can't I remember anything it does when it kicks in?"

"Listen, Mr. Zombie, I don't know anything. I'm telling you. I was just supposed to do the follow up psychology on you, what you remember, what you don't remember, to see if any of your memories come back. You know, psychology. All that surgery stuff and that chip, that is military and for the surgeon doctors, not me. I don't have anything to do with that. Look, all I know is I was supposed to evaluate you, give my report in....," he stopped suddenly.

I pressed my gun up against his forehead a little harder. "Give your report to who? Tell me exactly who and how."

"Listen, it was a long time ago. All that's changed and past. You disappeared without a trace."

"Nobody disappears without a trace. They've got a chip in my head," I said. But little did I know, they were using me to take out organized crime. Take down the big bosses and replace them with bosses they needed in there. When they got too big for themselves, they would be taken out, too. But what about the contracts on me?

The boss of bosses, the biggest crime lord of all. I had worked for him. It was a long time ago. I had enough stuff on him to put him away for good, just like I do most of the crime lords, but they got a lot on me, too, which makes it easy for them to live with themselves and not worry about me turning them in or even killing them. Blackmail, everybody had something on somebody, and nobody got by with nothing without paying for it. You rob a bank or any crime, you had to get permission. And you had to share the loot with the big boss or whoever is over the territory. I couldn't get anymore from the psychiatrist.

It wasn't long before I was on another job. The mob boss had a run in with the Russians, at least they talked Russian, but I know good and well they were born in the United States. I knew a couple of 'em, but my job was to take one down for some unknown reason. It must have been really bad. For the mob boss to want to go against the Russians was almost a crime against crime. If they all wipe each other out, there won't be no crime to organize. At least that's the way I felt about it.

That's when I got really got the nickname Zombie. I had been using it myself ever since the car accident I lived through. It seemed to fit, so I just stuck with it. Everybody got to thinking that I couldn't die.

It was the fourth floor up. I had just gotten off the elevator. Me and Knuckles, of course. I didn't know his real name. He was a little bigger than me, and everybody called him Knuckles, with good reason. One punch, and he'd kill a man. That's all it took. He would come around with a roundhouse coming downward right on the top of somebody's head. It would break their neck and fracture their skull. With one blow, they'd drop down to the ground. And that was gonna be the case as we stood before the door of Apartment 486.

Before I knocked, I asked my partner, "Hey Knuckles, why you think they got an eighty-six here? I don't see no eighty-six apartments on this floor. Do you?"

He looked down the hall, and then he looked the other way. "I don't know. Anything's possible."

"Knuckles, you never were too smart."

I knocked on the door. Tap. Tap. Tap. First, I went a little light. When I didn't hear anything, I pushed Knuckles behind me and waved my hand backward. When I did that, Knuckles backed up behind me. Just then, the wood flew off the door. Three bullets went whizzing by just as I expected.

I kicked the door. There he stood. The big ugly Russian stood right before me, a scar penetrating from the top of his forehead all the way to the bottom of his jaw. He had a patch on the other eye, nothing to do with the scar obviously. It was only then when he raised up a machine gun and let it rip. He didn't even get it raised before he started shooting.

As quick as I could, I put my foot on the side of the threshold of the door and pushed myself out in the hall. Sideways I went skidding down the hall. Knuckles was nowhere in sight. He got me. Both sides. Straight through my midsection. One on one side, and one on the other. It stung like fire. I felt the cool liquid flowing down my back, and then I felt it on my front.

Here he came, out the door. I stood up to my feet as fast as I could, looking for my gun. There it was behind him. I just looked at him while he walked toward me. He raised that machine gun up again. This time he took careful aim. When he pulled the trigger, nothing happened.

He threw the gun down and reached into his coat. Yeah, the big daddy of 'em all, a .357 Magnum, plastic tip, hollow point. He cocked the trigger and began to raise the gun up. It was a hair trigger. The gun went off before he got a chance to aim. It ricocheted off the floor right into my thigh. It blew a chunk of meat out of the back of my leg. I bent over and grabbed my leg.

I looked back up at him. He took careful aim at my head, and it was like it was slow motion. A flame came whizzing by the top of my head. Had I not been bent over, it would not have missed me as I looked as it passed. Every little detail. In slow motion.

It started from the top of his jaw in the front of his face. His bottom jaw just stayed there as his head fell backward. His face began to disappear from the top jaw bone all the way up to the forehead, scar and all. The flame went on past him. Right inside of the apartment's threshold, it hit the door. That's when it exploded.

Earlier on, I was supposed to meet Knuckles in front of the building, but little did I know, that outside the fourth floor on the stairwell of the fire escape, there was a rope tied, and at the end of it was a rocket launcher. Knuckles wasn't playing around. When I had told him to get out from in front of the door with the motion of my hand, he stepped out onto the fire escape, grabbed the rope, jerked the rocket launcher up, and turned around just in time to shoot Ugly right in the face.

When the bomb exploded, most of the percussion went into the apartment, but when it came back out, it blew the threshold, the door, everything across the hall into the wall. And as if that wasn't bad enough, it filled up the hallway. It was like an atomic explosion. It picked me up off my feet and slung me backward, and this is where it began to be spooky.

I went in slow motion past Knuckles. It's like we caught eye to eye as I flew by him in slow motion. Now that old building, somehow, someway, the fire escape banister got hooked on my foot as I whizzed by it. When it did, it slung me down instead of out. Next thing I knew, my arm was caught in the next fire escape banister pole, and when it did, it slung me in feet first down on the second floor of the fire escape. The percussion blew Knuckles back out on the fourth level of fire escape. Then he rolled back halfway down to the third level.

I was in shock to say the least. I didn't know what to think and what had just happened. I couldn't believe I was even alive. First, I looked down at my leg. Somehow the bleeding had stopped although I was quite bloody. My shirt was soaking wet, but the bleeding had stopped in every wound.

That's when I heard him. "Zombie," he said quietly.

"What?" I asked.

He said, "Zon, that's what you are, a zombie," as he looked down through the grade of the third floor down to the second floor where I was.

"What do you mean?" I asked.

"Zon Zombie, there's no way you could live after that." Now

he had been calling me that for a while, but this time, I could tell from the look on his face that he really believed it.

"What were you thinking?!?" I said to him.

"I saw you duck down," he said. "That was my chance. I didn't know it was gonna blow up the building. I just thought it was gonna kill him. Sorry."

"Sorry?!?!? Really?!?!? Is that all you have to say."

"Uhh... don't know what else to say."

"Great! Knuckles, come down here and help me get down this ladder," I said as I walked down the steps to the first level, thinking the whole time that that's all he had said about shooting me in the head. "Sorry." Now he was saying sorry again after blowing me up.

He helped me down the ladder with no problem at all. "Zombie," he said, "you ain't looking too good."

"Yeah, I ain't feeling too good either, buddy."

"Maybe I should take you where you need to go," he said as we headed toward his car.

"No, just get me to my car."

He said it again after he helped me in the car. "Zombie."

"Knuckles, why do you keep saying that?" It was the way he said it this time. It was different, almost scary. I looked in the mirror. My eyes were dark. My skin was pale. I was dying, if I wasn't already dead, which explained why he thought Zombie.

I woke up. I changed my clothes. I took a shower. I shaved. Scars, that's all they were. I got in my car, the blood stained seat, brown and ugly. I dreaded sitting in it. After I reached my destination, I got out with stains on the back of my jacket and the back of my trousers. The dried up blood had somewhat turned to powder. I wiped it off the best I could. I could still smell its dusty aroma as I headed up to the mob boss' office.

First, I walked by a couple of Knuckles' buddies. When I went in, they couldn't stop looking at me. There Knuckles was at the bottom of the steps, his eyes big. He took in a deep breath, looking at me eye to eye. He shook his head backward and forward as he shook a little bit. He wasn't too smart, but he was smart enough to know that in my condition, there was no way I could have lived.

The week I was out, Knuckles had spread the word how I had died, blown out of the window of the fourth floor of a Russian apartment building after I was shot three times. I didn't know that until I reached the next level and walked into the boss' office.

His mouth dropped open, "What?? You really are a zombie!"

"Excuse me?"

"Zon, the word is that you are dead after being shot up and blown up. The word is that you can't die now, huh?" He pulled out a .44 and aimed it straight at my heart.

I said, "Whoa, whoa, wait a minute now. That's crazy talk. I can die just like anybody else."

"Are you sure? You sure I don't need to test it?"

"I'm quite sure."

"Well, let's keep it that way. I got another job for you," he said.

"I can't do it. I've been shot up, blown up. I wake up a week later, not knowing what happened during that time."

"Zombie, maybe you died. Maybe you are a zombie after all.

102

But you just remember, you believe you can die, and that means I can kill you. And if you don't do what I say, that's exactly what I'm gonna do. I'm gonna kill ya. And you know me."

"Yeah, I know you. You won't kill me. You'll kill everybody I know, everybody I love."

But I knew that once I left his office, that was the last he was gonna see of me. So I played it off real smooth like. I said, "Okay, what's the job, being how I ain't got no choice? But you're gonna pay for the job this time, no more free work."

"Now Zombie, you owed me a lot of money. That's what got you into this mess in the first place."

That's when I told him the way I really felt. "That was many jobs ago since I paid that debt. The way I look at is you owe me now."

He pulled out an envelope with twenty thousand dollars in hundreds. He said, "That ain't the way I look at it. The way I look at it is that we're even. All them other jobs was the interest, but this job pays twenty thousand dollars. I want you to take out the head man of that dirty double crossing Russian."

I took my money and said, "Sure, we're even, like you said," as I went for the door.

He said, "Oh yeah, Zombie?"

I turned around and said, "Yeah?"

"Don't think about double crossing me."

But I got in my car and I drove, and I knew he wouldn't mess with my family because I didn't have any. And I knew he wouldn't mess with those that I love because his style was first he would capture me. But he wouldn't hurt anybody unless it was in front of

103

me, and I knew he wouldn't do nothing 'til he caught up with me. So I rented an apartment, and I spent my twenty thousand dollars very slowly and kept my profile very low.

It was almost nine months later when I heard a knocking on the door. I knew that knock. It went tap tap. Then, tap tap again. with a slight pause in the middle. I knew that was Knuckles. We had knocked on many doors. But this time, it wasn't as a friend. He was there to kill me. Now I knew old Knuckles wasn't very smart. He never went to school, and the little education he did have, well...he didn't.

But he wasn't alone. A man named Splow was with him. I asked him one time why they call him Splow. He said it was because he liked to take it nice and slow.

I said, "Really?"

He said, "Yeah, while I watch things explode. You get it?"

"Not really," I said.

We didn't much like each other because Splow liked to blow up people in their cars, not just a little bit. It was kinda like an art to him, and Knuckles had started hanging around him a year before that. That's where he got the rocket launcher. It's a wonder he didn't blow himself up when he got it, and he almost did anyway. Both of us.

I picked up my guns. I had a .357 and a .45, high grain, high powered bullets in 'em. I aimed 'em both at the door, and just for the fun of it, I made a loud sound like I thought a zombie would make. As soon as I stopped, the commotion started out in the hallway. I could hear him plain as day, "He's a zombie!"

"Zon ain't no zombie!" Splow told him.

That's when I opened fire. I emptied the guns out. I threw the .357 down, dropped the clip out of the .45, reached down under the sofa cushion, grabbed two other magazines, put one in the gun, chambered a bullet, and began firing again down the wall. I dropped that clip out and did the same thing. Only this time, I left half the bullets in the next magazine as I went to the door slowly. I reached for the doorknob.

Then, the doorknob jiggled. It turned a little bit at first, and then it turned a lot. Then I heard it click. As the door fell open, Knuckles was laying up against it face first. Now, he was lying down on the ground in the threshold.

That's when the edge of the threshold blew up right in my face. It was a bullet. I jumped back, plucking a splinter out of my cheek. I looked at the hole in the door that it had just made along with the other ones. Only this one was going straight through the other way.

Then I heard it. Click. Click. After wiping the blood off my cheek, I walked over to the door and looked out just a little bit. I saw a leg. It was on the ground. Then I looked some more. There he was. Splow was lying on the ground. I looked a little farther. His gun was pointing right at my head. I pulled back.

Click. Click. Click. I jumped out in the hallway and aimed carefully at his head. It was too late. He was dead.

"I gotta get out of here," I thought to myself, ranting and raging in the apartment, looking for my things as I was gonna get away. I had twelve thousand dollars left. All I had to do was go rent another apartment under an alias name.

I hated to see Knuckles lying there, but as I stepped back over his body, his eye blinked. I knelt down beside him and said, "Knuckles, you alive?"

I could barely understand him, with good reason. He was shot three times with a .357. Three little holes went in, but his back looked like hamburger where they came out. "They've got a contract on you."

"What? What'd you say?"

"Zombie, million dollars"

When I heard that, I knew that disappearing wasn't gonna be as easy as I thought it was now. But a million dollars? Why? That didn't make sense. Why would he care if I lived or died? Unless, of course.... I know. He thinks I'm gonna kill him.

That's when I knew what I had to do. It was gonna either be him or me. I reloaded my guns, put 'em away nice and careful like, and walked on out. Knuckles' eyes were still open when I walked by. I don't know if he died or if he lived. I wished him the best. I kinda liked him. When I got down on the first floor and walked out the door, I had the feeling that I was being watched.

I am careful to be very observant, cars, people in cars, vans, the way they park, SUVs. I've done private eye work before, so I knew what to look for. But somebody was watching me, and I knew it. It was a car down the road. I couldn't make out who it was.

I walked to the end of the sidewalk and turned to the right to walk down the road. That's when a car pulled up. A million thoughts went through my head as they demanded me to get into the car. I knew they weren't part of the underground terror. I've been running in this business long enough to know everybody.

The dirty cops picked me up and kept me for three months until I got tired of it.

That's how I ended up here.

As I think on all this, I know it is time to go. I have to leave the girl. I can't let her find out what I am. Zon Zombie.

9

Now the one thing I don't like is the fact that something's in my brain, and worse than that, it controls me in the worst way. It has been years, and everybody involved was taken out, the doctors, the nurses..... But what happened to the guy that I found at the doctor's house that had the surgery on his brain? What would they have done with his body? They wouldn't have buried him with a chip in his head.

On top of an old building, I stand there, pondering on the thought, but between the top of this building I am on and the top of the other building that is over fifty feet away, I step back with a theory in my head. "These old buildings love me."

So I take off running, and I jump. Now on the top of the edge of the buildings, there is a wall going around the top, some three feet, some two feet, some one. But as I leave the top of the building, the railing lifts me up, and as I glide over to the middle between the buildings, the railing comes off of the other side of the other building, gently grabs me, and pulls me over to it.

At first, I pause in astonishment as I look back. The old building, the railing goes back into place. Then I throw up again, the black stuff. Only it isn't as much this time. Instead of five or ten minutes of pure throwing up, it is just a few seconds. Whatever this stuff is coming out of my body, it doesn't look good.

Now with these old buildings saving me from any hurt or any harm, I get to thinking about that chip again. I jump off the side of the building, not knowing what to expect. The railing comes off of the fire escape, wraps around my waist, and gently lets me down to the cement.

I have been protecting these buildings my whole life, and now they're protecting me. I feel like a comic book character. Invincible, maybe. Indestructible. But then I touch my forehead. Maybe not.

I go to the hall of records. Finding nothing, but what am I looking for? I finally find the doctor's name. Dr. T. Dason, there he is. I open up the folder. Date of birth, nineteen something. Date of death, cause of death, cardiac arrest, heart attack. That's funny because I distinctively remember bullet holes in his head along with a few more in his body. Natural causes, I think not.

Then I go to the library, the newspaper. Dr. T. Dason dies of heart attack. Completely covered up. But what happened to the body of the hitman that was there? This is my answer. If I can find the body, I can find the chip that was in his head.

I go back to the doctor's house, new owner, a new doctor or lawyer, who knows, but it isn't there that I am going to find my answer. I go to some of the local houses. One in particular. An old woman comes to the door. "Yes can I help you?"

"I'm not sure if you can or not, ma'am. Do you remember Dr. Dason that lived down the road?"

"Well, yes I do. He was my doctor for a while. The funniest thing, he just up and died one morning. They say it was a heart attack, but I never said nothing to nobody about that."

"What do you mean?"

"Well, I was standing there at the gate along with about ten other people as they put him in that ambulance, and there was an awful lot of blood for a heart attack."

"Blood?"

"Yeah, the sheet they had him covered up with was just drenched in blood, but that's not the peculiar thing. It was the other body. They put him in a white van and drove off."

"A white van? Ma'am, did it have any writing on it?"

"No, but there was an emblem on the side of the van. It was green. Diamond shaped, I do believe, but in the middle of it, it looked like green plants coming out of it."

"Green plants, what do you mean?"

"Well, there were six leaves, three on each side as it came out of the diamond. Here, I'll draw you a picture."

After she comes back with a pen and piece of paper, she quickly draws the diagram that was on the side of the van. I've never seen this before, but I have a feeling this is the answer that I am looking for.

"Is there anything else you can remember, ma'am? Anything at all?"

"Why is it so important to you?" the old woman asks.

"I believe the doctor was murdered."

That's when she looks at me and pushes me back a little bit from in front of the screen door. Then she pulls the screen door to and puts the little lock on it, and before she shuts the main door, she says, "Murdered, you said?" She looks at me real close.

She knows something, but getting it from her isn't going to be easy. She says, "Mind yourself. Or you may end up just like the doctor."

"Yeah, why is that?" I ask, my voice getting stern, and anger filling my conscience as I think about it.

"Well, I'm gonna tell you why, those blood stained sheets that I saw is the reason I haven't said anything for all these years, and then you show up at my door. Don't think I didn't see you coming from that house. I was sitting right here on the porch when I saw you drive by in the good doctor's car. Yeah, you're older now. You gonna kill me, too?" Then she slams the door.

Well, it was true. I drove right out the gates, right by the old woman's house. She knew the doctor's car, and I looked straight at her as I passed by. I step down off the porch.

She opens the front door back up. As I start walking down her sidewalk to leave, she yells out, "So you're not here to kill me?"

"No ma'am, and I didn't kill the doctor either, but the man that killed him, I did kill." And then I left. I don't know if that comforted her any. I'm sure it does.

I hold up the piece of paper the old woman gave me. I begin

to ask around. Nobody knows anything. I go to the local library again and get on a computer. Emblems of businesses. I go through hundreds of them. My eyes begin to sting and water. Then, the thought comes to me. Military. Military incorporations, emblems. It narrows it down quite a bit. There are only about three hundred or so.

I finally find it. It is the Dry Corp. Hyperchip technology. An address and a phone number. I quickly write them down, but when I call the number, the operator says I have reached a number in error, to check the number and redial. After three times, I go back to the computer to make sure I wrote the number down right. As far as the address, it is in the Alps, a long way from where I am. I can go there, but it will take a long time. I'm afraid the address won't be real and that I'll be wasting my time.

There I am, once again, on top of a building. Looking across the city. I notice right as it begins to get dark, a green emblem on a building far away, way on the other side of the city. I can't make it out at first, but when I remember the old woman saying it was green leaves, I think to myself, "It can't be." I have to investigate.

I jump from old building to old building, heading toward the green emblem that I think... it is a long shot, but as I jump from old building to old building, I reach the new buildings uptown. After the old building lets me off onto the new building, I go to jump to the next building that is only twenty feet away. The new buildings don't help me. Neither will they save me. That explains the gun shot to the head.

I still have a long way to go, but this time, I have to take the sidewalk. That's when I see the emblem again on the side of the building, the big, tall skyscraper. Only this time, it is plain as day, a diamond with three green leaves on each side coming out of the center of it, folding over on top of the diamond.

When I get to the building, the doors are locked. The lights are on on the first floor. Two security guards sit at a desk. I tap on the window. They look at me, and then they ignore me. I tap harder. They still ignore me.

I am tired, and the night has grown long. I grab a hotel and bed down for the night. "I'll get up nice and early in the morning," I say to myself.

With no buzzer to wake me up, I quickly look at my watch. After murmuring and talking under my breath, I get up. It's nine thirty. I wanted to get up at six, although I needed the extra sleep, the five and a half hours of sleep that I got. I quickly get back to the building. The same guards. Sitting at the same desk. This time, I bang harder. The doors are still locked. They still ignore me.

I see two other guards walking down the hall straight up to the desk. They shake the other guards' hands, exchange places, and the other guards walk down the hall. But where did they go? I walk around the building. There is no back door. It is solid, solid glass all the way around. Only the glass gets darker on the side and the back. But how did they get in? How did they get out?

I'm puzzled. I walk around and try to figure it out for hours. It is almost one. My stomach is growling, and I am thirsty, too. There is a nearby cafe. After refreshments and a good meal, I sit there, patiently drinking my coffee. How are they getting in? How are they getting out? I go to the restroom and empty out the coffee and go back to my seat. After six cups of coffee, I am a little bit anxious, to say the least. I hadn't noticed the people that had come in.

"Yeah, I've got to pull a double tonight," I hear.

"That'll be the third time this week, won't it?" the waitress says.

"Yeah, after this, it will be straight time. They are hiring some new guards."

My eyebrow raises up. I turn around, and there he sits, one of the guards I had seen earlier that morning and earlier on before that. "My patience has paid off," I think to myself.

Just then, the man yells out. He has spilled coffee all over himself. "Oh, you poor thing," the waitress says, "Let me help you with that," as she takes a napkin and begins to wipe the coffee up.

The man curses with anger in his voice. "I've got to go back to the house now, change my trousers."

I laugh. Trousers, that's what you call 'em alright. Most full blooded Americans think of them as pants.

He gets up and walks out of the door. "Sir," the waitress yells.

"Yeah, what do you want?"

"You forgot to pay."

He throws ten dollars on the counter." Keep the change," he says as he does every day he comes in there. "I'll see you later."

She smiles and says, "Have a nice day. Thanks for the tip."

I walk up to the register. "How much?"

"Two eighty."

I lay down a five and walk out of the door. I hear her saying something, but I don't make it out. The door shuts too soon. But I'm too late. He has disappeared, and I don't have a car.

That's when he comes around the corner, Mercedes Benz. Wow, he's doing well for himself, a Mercedes Benz. It isn't the most expensive Mercedes. It's the cheaper one, but still, it is more than a guard should make, by far.

There is a taxi coming down the road. I step out in front of it. "Taxi!"

"I've got a fare," the driver says.

I quickly open the door and hop in. "I'll pay your fare. I'll pay my fare, and I'll give you double."

The man in the backseat says, "Well, Mister, you've got yourself a deal."

The driver says, "I don't know if you wanna do that. I've been driving this nut around all morning."

"Yeah, it's true, Mister. I've been sightseeing all day long. Me and this driver's become quite good friends."

"That's all fine and dandy. Follow that Mercedes right there."

That's when the man in the backseat clams up, seeing how serious I am.

"Don't let him get out of sight, but don't let him know you're following him," I say.

The smiles wipe off their faces. I throw a couple of hundreds on the front seat. "This oughta cover the cab drive."

After ten minutes of following him, he pulls up into the suburbs. Not the rich neighborhood, but just on the suburbs of the rich neighborhood. They are very wealthy and very nice houses. I see the Mercedes pull into a drive way. "Pull over here," I say.

115

"What now, Mister?"

"Just wait."

The guy in the backseat says, "I think I'll just get out here."

"Sit still, you," I tell him.

The Mercedes backs back out of the drive way and takes off in a hurry. "Quick, get after him!"

The cab driver says, "I don't think I can keep up with him."

"Well, he's going back the general direction we just came from. Just keep that in mind."

So as he loses him around the next block, he knows to turn back, and as soon as he does, there he is. "Floor it!" I tell him.

The cab driver gives it all he can give it. But running stoplights, trying to keep up, he loses him. I see the tail end of the car as we go by as it goes into an underground car lot. "Stop here!" I throw another hundred dollars down. "Thanks for the ride." As I get out, the man in the backseat wipes the sweat off his face and exhales as he is relieved that I have gotten out of the car.

I walk down the walkway of the parking lot. The guard disappears into the dark. But as I make my way down, the darkness begins to clear out as the lights start to light the way. Looking down through the cars, I don't see the Mercedes, so I begin to jog a little ways. After I get halfway down, I can see the next level going downward. There it goes. Four levels down.

I wonder to myself what this place is. After going down four levels, I finally see the car. It is empty. The back wall has an elevator. I have to act quickly. There are no numbers, no lights, just a round button beside the elevator with no light in it. It is just a stainless steel badge that you push.

After pushing the elevator door button, I wait for a few moments. Nothing happens. I push the button again. Nothing happens.

Another car shows up. Now down through the center of this parking lot, there are big columns. Two on this end, and two on the other. When I see the car coming, I quickly get behind one of the columns. I know where the car is going because there is only one empty spot. As soon as he pulls in, he gets out of the car murmuring, "Man I'm gonna have to hurry. I'm gonna be late."

He takes a badge and places it in front of the button. As soon as the door opens, he quickly goes in. The door shuts quickly, and he disappears.

"This is going to be tougher than I thought," I think. I walk back up and go out of the parking lot. When I get back up to the sidewalk, I walk down to the end of the block. It is quite a ways. I look across the street. The building takes up the whole block. But it is the back of it. I cross the street and walk around, and then I walk to the front of the building, to where the doors are. They are big, tall glass doors, and there they sit, two guards, the same desk. I bang harder this time. One of the guards comes to the door with his hand on a gun pointing with his left hand. "Go away from the door!" he says.

It isn't ten minutes later when I bang on the door again. "Go away from the door!" he yells again.

A policeman pulls up outside of the building and then another one. They jump out of their cars with their hands on their guns. "Sir, step away from the building, please! What's your business here?"

"I'm trying to get a job. I was told to come to this address."

"What address?"

"To be honest with you, I can't remember, but I was told this big tall building on the four hundredth block."

"Well sir, this isn't the four hundred block."

"Yeah, it is. It's right here on the sign, four hundred."

"Sir, that's four thousand. You're uptown. What you're looking for is a long ways away from here."

"Well, it's a logical mistake. Why don't they open the door and tell me that?" I say, begruntled.

"Sir, if you don't leave, we're going to have to take you in. You've got your choice. Go to jail, or go on about your business."

"Well, I'll be about my business, I guess. Why do they have those doors locked in the middle of the day anyway? It looks like they would have just told me I was at the wrong building."

I look through the glass one more time as I walk away slowly. Here two more guards come, the one that I had followed, switching places again, no doubt pulling his double, but this time, I know the shift. It's nine o'clock. The shifts change every twelve hours. But this guy is going to pull a double shift. All I have to do is go back to the cafe after a good night's sleep and wait for him to show back up.

"Dang, this is taking longer than I thought," I think as I sit there at the cafe the next day. Six cups of coffee. Still no guard. It's eight o'clock. Still hasn't shown up. Ten after nine. It's a waste of time.

I get up out of the booth, and there he comes through the door. He looks tired and worn out. He was supposed to get off at nine that morning. I have been at that cafe all day. My stomach is full, and so is my bladder. After going to the restroom, I sit back down in my booth.

Here comes the waitress. "Well, you've been here all day, haven't you? You were here before my shift."

"Yeah, I'm waiting on somebody."

"Well, I get off in a minute. I've got a feeling they ain't gonna show up."

My eyes get big. "Well, you sure got a lot of patience," she says as she walks off.

"What'll you have?" she asks him.

"I don't know. I'm tired, sleepy, hungry, and thirsty."

"Why you so tired?"

"I just pulled a double. I told you that yesterday."

"Yeah, I can't remember everything everybody says," she says to the man.

As I had sat there all day, I had tried to remember things. That's when my mind goes back to when Knuckles told me he shot me. Something isn't right about that.

As I had waited, I had remembered even more, back even further than I've ever remembered before. When I was a teenager, I had somewhat of a mentor, well, not really a mentor at all. I never had a problem speaking my mind, and it was my first job. The first day on the job, it was an old warehouse. The old supervisor was in his sixties, maybe even seventies, if he didn't look older than that, and by the sound of his voice, well, let's just put it this way, there were no pleasantries in it at all. But I could hear that old man barking orders to the employees that were already working.

"Move that crate over here, you little sidewinder," he said to another employee that had just started working a couple of weeks ago.

He made his way to the big doors. Seeing me standing there, he barked at me. "What's your problem, young man? Did you come to work or are you just going to stand there? You start at the bottom just like everybody else. Grab that broom over there and start sweeping."

Now I didn't say a word. I held my peace quietly, but as I stood there, my anger grew, listening to the old man barking orders, saying, do this, do that. He wasn't doing it to me as bad yet, but I knew it wouldn't be long until he started treating me the same way.

By the time lunchtime came, I was so filled with energy from the excitement of getting a new job that I decided to work through lunch, and for the past five hours, I had been sweeping on that old warehouse. Five big piles. I swept over half the warehouse. The old man was late taking lunch, but after everybody else was already gone, he finally made his way to the lunchroom.

I could hear him grumbling about the trash on the floor. "That new boy ain't done nothing but make a mess. It's worse now than when he started sweeping."

Now when I heard that, I just kept on working, but I had already made up my mind that I was going to put the old man in his place when he came back out if he said anything to me at all. But by the time lunch hour was over, I had already gotten the five big piles of swept up stuff up, bagged up, and put away in its proper place, and with the warehouse over halfway swept, well, that's more than anybody had ever done in one week much less half a day's work. And it was good. It wasn't none of that half sweep up and go about your business. I swept and swept and swept five or six times in the same spot until every bit of the dirt was gone. Half the warehouse.

Now when the old man came out of lunch, wondering if I had quit because he didn't see me in the lunchroom, I started on the other half of the warehouse. Another pile. Here the old man came. "Look here, young fella, you're making a damn mess all over the warehouse."

"You listen here, you old fart, you think you're going to talk to me the way you're talking to those other guys, you've got another thing coming."

"What?!?"

"You heard me, old man. You better get some respect for me right now if you know what's good for you."

"Respect?!? Son, look around you. We're in a warehouse. The only respect I've ever got was dust, black carbon, and a week paycheck, and I don't mean once a week. I mean weak, like in not enough pay."

"Old man, you know what you need?"

"Well, I got a feeling you ain't gonna be the one to give it to me, young fella," he said with a hateful tone in his voice.

I walked right up to him and gave him a big hug, almost picking the old man up off the ground. When he realized I wasn't hurting him, his expression changed on his face. The old man was in shock. "What are you doing, young fella?"

"All you need is a friend, you old fart, somebody that ain't gonna take your shit."

When I backed away from him, a big smile came on his face. "You ain't never had a friend before, have you, old man?" I asked.

"Nope, I don't reckon I have. I ain't never had much use for 'em."

"You and me both. But you and I have to work together. That means we're gonna get an understanding right now. If you want me to do something for you, I'll be glad to do it, but you're gonna ask me to do it."

I put my arm around his shoulders. "Now look here, I wanna show you what I've been doing." I took him to the back corner of the warehouse. I borrowed his flashlight that he took off his belt and shined it on the floor.

When the old supervisor saw the floor, he saw it was clean enough to eat off of, and when he saw that the five big piles that were in the middle of the warehouse on each aisle were all cleaned up, he couldn't believe it. I had done this during lunch hour. The old man said, "You know something, that's the best anybody's ever done on these floors. Usually when I tell them to sweep, they come over here and half heartedly look like they're sweeping until I tell them to do something else."

Now with that floor clean like it was, that old man had done gained respect for me. He knew I wasn't one to toy with, and he knew he could trust me. The old man loved me. We worked together for a long time. It wasn't long before I moved up to his place. "Yeah, I'm retiring next week. I'll be teaching you how to supervise. You're gonna take my place," he said.

I didn't know, and neither did the old man, but the crates that had been coming in for the last few months, well, they had been targeted by the CIA, ATF, FBI, and a bunch of other federal agents. The goods were smuggled in from ships from out of the country, towed in on a truck, and stored at this warehouse.

"Four days until retirement," the old man said.

Here came three big trucks. One backed up to the pallet loading dock at the back of the building, and two drove inside. The one outside was to make it look legitimate. As they unloaded the goods, it was pretty smart the way they did it. They would take the cases of legitimate goods and make a wall around those that weren't legitimate, smuggled drugs, guns, whatever it was. So if one of the crates was to get opened up, it would be on the outside wall, which no doubt would be a bunch of legitimate goods.

It was nine o'clock in the morning. I looked up and heard helicopters. "What do you think that is?" I asked the old man.

"I don't know, but it don't sound good."

That's when all the doors busted open. You could hear agents all through the warehouse. "ATF, get your hands up!"

"FBI!"

The old man carried a crowbar. This made it easy to move the crates that were too close together. He would just throw that old crowbar in there and move the corner of the crates, and the forklift would be able to move the crates on up into a slot. Now from the back, FBI agents came in, and then they came in from the front, and a few came around the crates with their guns just a pointing at, well, at anybody that stood there. And there the old man stood by the crates that he had just got through straightening up.

"Drop it," one of the agents said as he pointed his gun at the old man.

He already had one hand up, and I had my hands up, wondering what was going on, but when he heard the agent say to drop it, the old man dropped that crowbar. It hit the fork on the forklift. Being dark in that section of the warehouse, darker than others, it made a loud bell like sound and it sparked, and with the old man's back to the agent, being young and ignorant like the agent was, he just let it go.

I grabbed my leg as I hit the floor. When I looked down, the old man laid on the ground. I pulled myself over to him. I was breathing heavy, heavier than usual. It wasn't the pain from the shot in my leg. It was my friend lying there taking his last breath.

The supervisor of the agent came up behind him. "What happened?" he asked.

"I thought he had a gun."

"What have you done?"

"I thought he was going to shoot me."

I looked up at him. "He was unarmed. We all are. We're just warehouse workers. That's all we are."

The old man took in his last breath and breathed out. My heart got heavy, so heavy I couldn't even hold my head up. But when I pulled my hand out from my leg, it was soaked in blood.

"Quick, call an ambulance," the head agent said as the other agents gathered around.

"There's nothing here!" some of the agents cried out. "The

cases have no guns, no weapons of any type. They're just VCRs and televisions, junk. It's all legitimate."

That's when everything went black. But waking up in the hospital two days later, I heard, "We almost lost you," as I came out of a deep sleep. "You lost a lot of blood. You've been in a coma for a little while." It was a young nurse. She wasn't much to look at, and she didn't sound too pleasant either.

"What happened?" I asked her.

"Well, you lost over a quart of blood, and you almost died. There's an agent standing outside waiting for you to come out of a coma. They're gonna want to talk to you."

"Well, I don't want to talk to them. Matter of fact, they can go to blazes for all I care, and you can tell them I said so. They killed my best friend, and shot me up, about killing me. How come I feel cold and weak?"

There was a bag of blood hanging up on a steel post, along with a white bag. It was clear. They were going straight into my veins. "Well, after that last bit of blood gets into your body, that will probably warm you up. We didn't know why you were in a coma."

"Yeah, why was I in a coma? I was just shot in the leg."

We thought that, too, when you first came in, but after we got your leg sewed up, you were still losing blood. You were shot in the belly, but the entry wound almost closed up after the bullet went in."

"Well, that's unusual, don't you think?"

She said, "Yes, it is unusual. But for the last couple of days, we've been trying to find the bullet wound."

"You mean for two days, you couldn't find a bullet hole?"

"To be honest with you, we never did find the bullet hole, but we took an x-ray of your belly. First, we took x-rays of your head and then your chest, both of your legs, then your belly. We got the bullet out alright, but we have no idea how it got in your belly."

"What was all the bleeding?"

"It hit your liver."

"That's not good."

"No, that's never good. But it was just on the edge. Just enough to make you bleed out slowly."

"Well, I take it you got me all fixed up then, huh?"

An agent stuck his head in the door. "Ah, you're awake, are you?"

Then he shut the door, and then a few minutes later, here two of them came back, not the same one that had stuck his head in the door. "Listen, young man, we need to ask you some questions."

"The only questions you're gonna ask me is how to get out of here, and that door's the only way you're gonna get. I've got nothing to say to you coppers."

"We're federal agents, not coppers."

"Murderers is what you are, you along with that gun happy agent. He murdered my best friend in cold blood."

"That was an accident," he said as he called me by my name, but I couldn't remember it. I could remember every detail other than that. I remember how it felt. My heart was growing hard, and I was getting colder.

But as I laid there in the bed thinking about the old man, I thought about how mean and hateful he was when I had started working there, but before long, he was saying yes sir and no sir, mr this and mr that to the employees. The employees weren't late for work or laying out because they no longer had a hard boss to work for.

But the agents persisted. "Listen, young man, it would be better if you cooperate."

"There's nothing to cooperate with. The warehouse is a legitimate business. You all raided it and murdered people."

"Like I said, that was an accident," the agent said.

"Why are you still here? I asked you to leave."

"Well, listen, about the lawsuit...."

"What lawsuit?"

"Well... you're gonna sue us, right?"

"I never said I was suing anybody."

"What about your hospital expenses?"

"Well, I didn't put me in here. You did. So you pay the hospital."

Now seeing the tension ease out of their faces when they realized they weren't getting sued, the head agent spoke up and said, "We'll be getting in touch with you, but as far as that warehouse goes, they're smuggling drugs, guns, and anything else they choose to. We don't know how they're doing it....."

"Lies, all lies. Now get outta here. I don't wanna hear no more of your lies. You're just trying to cover up for the murder of my dearest friend, and as far as seeing me again, I don't think that would be wise. Or I might change my mind about that suing. I hope we see eye to eye."

As the agent disappeared into the hallway, the other agent said to him, "Man he's a real smart ass."

The other agent replied as they walked down the hallway, "No, he's right. We murdered a man in cold blood. That old man had been working there his whole life. He ain't never been in trouble and ain't never caused no trouble, and the agent that shot him, well, it ain't looking good for him. That's all I've got to say."

"Yeah, I heard he got suspended," he said as their voices faded away.

I looked up at that blood bag. It was empty, then I looked down at my leg. Then I raised up the gown and saw the big old scar on my belly. "I thought ya'll couldn't find the entry for the bullet that was in my belly. Why did they cut a hole in me so big?" I asked the nurse.

"Sir, I don't know why they did that, but from what I hear, they couldn't find the bullet, so they had to cut you open a little farther than they normally would. It was halfway in your liver and then they thought infection set in and they had to wait for you to stabilize. After you got out of recovery, we still couldn't get you awake, so they moved you into here, into this room."

I reached down and took the needles out of my arm. "I've had a pleasant stay, but it's time to leave."

"Sir, you can't do that!"

"Oh yeah, I just did it."

She walked out of the room briskly, yelling for the doctor at the nurse's station, "Doctor, come quickly!"

I didn't see my clothes at first. I opened a cabinet up. There they were in a plastic bag, along with my shoes and everything else. The pants and shirt were drenched in blood.. As I slipped my shirt on, I saw a hole in the shirt, right where my wound was. One hole in, no hole out. Now those pants were stiff as a board with that dried up blood on there, and as soon as I slipped them up, here came the doctor.

"What are you doing?" he asked.

"I'm leaving. That's what I'm doing."

"Sir, you're in no condition to leave. You won't even make it out of the hospital before you pass out."

"That's what you think. Now move to the side. I don't wanna have to get rough with you, and don't call security because I don't want to hurt anybody," I said as I looked dead into the doctor's eyes. "You the one that did the surgery on me?"

"That's right."

"Well, thanks," I said as I walked out of the door.

Now when I got to the hospital door, the entryway, I started feeling a little fuzzy, then I got to thinking about what the doc said. "Maybe he's right. Maybe I shouldn't leave," I thought. Then I thought about my dead buddy. The dizziness left. Anger filled my heart.

It was another warehouse deal not long ago as I stood there, thinking about who I was looking at. It was the same agent that had killed my buddy, but this time, he wasn't raiding the place. He was protecting it. He was working for his own boss. A dirty cop. A dirty agent. They're all the same. They're criminals. They deserve what they get, just like the rest of the criminals.

Now I stood there as I looked at the agent. I was perplexed. "My life might have went a different way had it not been for this agent," I thought as I looked at him. I hadn't remembered the old man until just then. It was the most I had remembered so far, the farthest back.

But as they unloaded a crate of guns, the top of the corner clipped another box, knocking the top of the side off. Some guns fell out on the floor. The agent looked at me, "Mr. Zombie, come over here and help me pick these guns up."

I walked closer. His face hit the light. The man was a lot older, and so was I. He stood up. "You're not Zon Zombie."

"That's right, you dirty copper." I pulled out my gun, and before the agent could even shoot his gun, I had done shot him six times. "That's for killing my friend."

Then I stood over him and shot him again, "And that's for shooting me."

Now when the other guys saw this agent lying dead on the ground and me standing over him, the guy got off the forklift and said, "The boss ain't gonna like this, Zon, you killing that federal agent like that."

"Yeah, what was I supposed to do, let him shoot me? He already did that. He should have finished the job long ago."

The guy stood there. His eyes got big. But he knew the dirty agent had it coming to him. He had been covering up killings for years, taking cuts, blackmail, bribes, you name it. I didn't know his name, but I never forgot a face, even one scarred up, and even with the memory loss. But standing there, I remembered everything but still not my own name.

"Zon, that agent knew you."

"Yeah, I just didn't want to be dead before he said who I was.

Besides I've done been told who I was, years ago, and none of that matters anyway. I'm a different person."

Now that old warehouse, there was something funny about it. I made sure it was kept clean for years, but peculiar things happened while I was there supervising.

The first thing that happened is that a mob boss gave me a visit. It was after I got shot. Here he came, walking in. He called me by name, my full name. "Listen, I've been hearing stories."

"Yeah, what kinda stories?"

"Well, I heard that you fell off that platform up there, and when the guys came over to where you were at and should have been dead, you stood there. How did that happen?"

"I've got no idea what you're talking about."

"Listen, some of the guys think you're invincible. You've been shot. You fell off platforms. How is it that you're still alive? Things have fallen off on top of you and missed you. My boys have given me all the info. It seems to me, mister.....," he went on as he said my name.

I stood there, wondering what he wanted, so I got got to the point. "What do you want?" I asked.

"Well, I'm gonna tell you like it is. I could use a man with your talent, and you can make a lot of money while I do."

"I've got plenty of money."

"Yeah, you got enough to make it, enough to pay on an apartment, drive an old car, ten years old, matter of fact, nothing to look at, and that apartment you live in, well, no civilized person would even go in there."

"You been in my apartment?"

"Oh yeah, I checked you out very carefully."

"I'm not sure I'm too pleased about that. And you said nobody civilized would go in there. What does that make you?"

"Oh, I'm not civilized at all. Matter of fact, you're gonna find working for me quite uncivilized. You see, all this is mine. This warehouse and ten others like it. And you, like all the rest of the employees, work for me whether you like it or not. Now word is you owe a lot of money."

"Yeah, I got shot up a few years ago."

"Yeah, I know. You were working for me when you got shot." I didn't know I was working for the mob until I did a little investigating about what we had been storing at the warehouse.

"I tell you what I'm gonna do. You're gonna be one of my regular hands. I tell you to do something. You go do it, and I pay you, but as far as all the payments to the hospital...."

"There ain't no payments. I borrowed the money to pay them off, over fifty thousand dollars."

"How come you didn't sue like everybody else does?"

"That ain't my way. Besides, I don't like lawyers. And I don't like courtrooms."

"Well, that's something we've got in common. I took the liberty of paying the other boss off that you borrowed the money from. Why did you even pay off the doctors and the hospital anyway? I wouldn't have done it."

That's when I remembered. She was young and beautiful. It wasn't long after I got out of the hospital when I ran into the ugly nurse at a local bar. She introduced me to her friend. It was love at first sight. I couldn't take my eyes off of her.

132

"So you work at the hospital?"I asked her.

"Yes, I work in accounting. You know, you owe almost fifty-three thousand dollars?"

"Yeah, I wouldn't doubt it. I was there only a couple of days, expensive motel. Don't you think?"

"One of the best."

After talking a while, we fell in love. Every spare moment we spent together. But with me working at the warehouse and her working at the hospital, we only had a couple of hours a night to spend with each other.

But today, she had a smile on her face. Not the usual smile that she usually had. She called me by my name and told me how much she loved me, and then she told me what she had done. She had paid off the hospital. Money she had saved from the time she went to work. She kept saying my name over and over again as she told me she loved me.

"Why would you do that?" I asked her.

"Well, I thought it was obvious. I want to spend the rest of my life with you."

"But I had no intentions of paying that hospital off. But you, you been saving that money for a long time."

"It's just money."

"Well, I could have thought of a lot better things to do with it than to give it to the hospital. That's all."

Soon after that, I was working, and a truck came in. The driver came up to me, "Man, today's my last job. I finally got my mob boss paid off."

"What do you mean?" I asked.

He said, "Well, I had to borrow one hundred thousand dollars ten years ago, and today I'm paid up, two hundred and twenty thousand dollars I had to pay back. But I'm telling you one thing, it sure feels good."

"Yeah, who did you borrow the money from?"

"Like I told you, my boss loaned it to me."

"I never thought about asking my boss for such a large sum of money."

"Well, you can go to my boss. He'll loan it to you, but it ain't cheap at one hundred and ten percent payback."

"Wow, that ain't cheap. Why don't you take me to your boss?"

"Sure, hop in. We'll go see him right now."

"Now Mister, I just wanna tell you, if you don't pay this money back, what's going to happen to you, your friends, your family," the mob boss said.

"It's just me, no family, no friends."

"Oh, I'll find somebody you love. Now fifty-three thousand dollars, you're going to owe me quite a bit after this. It's daily compound interest. You know that right? Why do you have to borrow this much money anyway?"

"I've gotta pay a friend back."

"I thought you didn't have friends."

"Well, I don't. I broke up with her."

"Ah, female problems."

"No problem at all. Come to think of it, after I give her this money, that will be the end of my problems."

There I stood in the doorway with the money in my hands. "Here's all the money you spent on the hospital."

"I don't want it," she said. "I did that because I love you. I still love you, and I'll be here when you get ready for me, if you ever do."

"Look, take this money."

"No, I'll never take that money. I can't take this money. Listen, I need to tell you something. The hospital gets donations every year, and I took some of the donated money and applied it to your account. That's what I do in accounting. I'm sorry I led you to believe that I paid it off."

That's when some of my memory went blank as to what happened, but there I was, back in that mob boss' office again. "Here's your fifty-three thousand dollars back. I don't need it."

"Now look here, Mister," he said as he called me by my name, "a deal's a deal. You borrowed the money. Now you still owe me seventy thousand dollars."

"I didn't even borrow the money for twenty-four hours."

"I don't care. When you walked out of that door, that was the contract. You knew the business. Now why are you playing dumb all of the sudden?"

As I laid down the money on the table and walked out, he said my name for the last time and said, "Don't forget, seventy-two thousand dollars. I'll give you adequate time, but after that, I'm gonna come collecting that money."

That's how it all started, I guess.

At the cafe, after scarfing down food and a cup of coffee and a half of a glass of water, the guard gets up and walks out, but this time I am ready for him. My car is parked out in front. Now with a good night's sleep and a car ready to go, I just follow him back to his house, and there I park out in front down the road a ways.

I am sound asleep when I hear a tap on the window. "Mister, you can't park here."

"What? What'd you say?"

"You're parked in front of my house. You can't park here. I've got four cars. My wife comes home, parks in the driveway. My son comes home, parks in the driveway. Now you're in my parking space. Move your ass."

"Look, I don't wanna get smart with you."

He backs up from the window and holds up his hands. "Okay, take it easy. I don't want no trouble. I just want my parking space. This is my house. Why are you parked here anyway? Oh, the hell with it." He gets in his car and parks in front of mine. There the guard goes out of his driveway. I crank my car up and slowly drive up as the man gets out of his car. "Now you move it, he yells. "Asshole!"

"Yeah, it takes one to know one, I guess," I think as I slowly drove down the road. This time, I know where I'm going. I park outside of the parking lot. Down the ramp I go. After a brisk run and a brisk jog and a fast walk, there I stand in front of the elevators. Just in time. Here comes the car, the Mercedes Benz. Back behind the column I go.

I think to myself how poor the security is. But as soon as that badge hits that button, I am on top of him. Into the elevator we go. "Sir, you can't come in here." He reaches for his gun. But when he feels and there is nothing there, he remembers he doesn't put his gun on until he gets to where he is going, and that is where I need to be.

"Listen, I've got some questions for you," I tell him.

I look at his forehead. He says, "What are you looking at?"

"Have you had any surgeries in your head?"

"No, why do you ask?"

I say, "Oh nothing. Then I punch him in the nose as hard as I can. He just slides down the wall down beside the elevator buttons. There are no numbers. Apparently he has already pressed the buttons that he needed to get where he was going.

But this elevator doesn't go up or down. The doors open, a large hallway. "That's peculiar," I think. It is the building that I couldn't get in. I poke my head out of the elevator and think, "What, no cameras, nothing?"

But this is just the first floor of a secured building, and this is just for the guards. There is an office over across the hall as I exit the elevator. It is a locker room, and a guard is getting dressed. "Oh, you must be a new guy," he says as I walk in.

"Yeah."

"Dang, you look pretty rough. Usually they hire young good looking guys like me," he smiles while he is saying it.

"Oh, you're a real comedian, aren't you?"

"Yeah, that's me. All fun and games. I like to have a little fun, don't you?"

"What exactly are we guarding anyway?" the guard asks after a moment.

"I don't know. You ever been on the upper floors?"

"You know, there are no upper floors from this floor."

"What exactly do you mean?"

"There's no way into this building at all, as far as we know.

137

Even our coming in is secretive. You've seen the parking lot. It's over a block away. There's no way in, and no way out. Even those glass doors out there, they don't even work. How is that, downtown, a building that can't be entered or exited? I will tell you this. Helicopters come in the morning, and they come in the afternoon. Three of 'em, one after another."

This guard obviously likes to talk. So that's how they're doing it. That's when I punch him in the face, take his badge, and go back across the elevator. All this time wasted, listening to the waitress waiting on people, watching these silly guards do nothing. What are they guarding? Nothing. Decoys, that's all they are.

I go to the building across the street. Yeah, it is higher. I make my way up to the roof. It isn't as easy as I thought it would be, but there I stand on the roof, waiting for those helicopters. Here they come. Six oh five. One after another one. The helicopter launch pad fills up with a handful of people. They look real important.

After the helicopters fill up, one by one, they take off. With two lanes going and two lanes coming down at the road, the buildings are too far apart for me to jump, but I have no choice. I go plumb across to the other side of the building and begin to run. It is a hundred feet higher than the other building. Right before I get to the end, I stop and take off running. When I get to the edge of the building to where I am supposed to jump, I chicken out, almost not stopping in time.

This building doesn't pick me up like the other ones did. I look down at the side of this building. Fifty feet lower, there is a ladder on the side. I go over to investigate. Now fifty feet across

138

and fifty feet down, that makes more sense to me, so I climb down to the other roof. Then I run.

As hard as I can, I run and I jump with all my might. I look down as I go over cars. Horns blowing. People walking. Down I go, faster and faster. Then my feet hit the building. I roll ten or fifteen feet and then skid on my back and my belly. Another twenty feet. I know I'm busted up. I have to be. But after a few seconds of not feeling pain, I can feel the wounds healing themselves.

I throw the black stuff up again. It is a small pile this time. Way smaller than any of the others. Whatever is in my body, I am getting to the end of it. I can see why the building didn't have so much security. The only way in is by helicopter.

After looking at these titanium doors I stand before, I see a little room to the side of them that you step into. There it has a pad for your hand, a retinal scan, and a little thing that pricks your blood to see your blood type and do a DNA scan. Each person has to pass through this room, and after all are scanned in, the big titanium doors are opened after the doors to the room shut.

I step up to the retinal scan. It does nothing. I put my hand on the pad. It does nothing. Nothing works there. I am now stuck on top of a building, hundreds of feet above the streets. I know I won't live if I fall from this height, and I know the helicopters won't bring people back until six in the morning.

I go over to the helicopter pad. There is a small opening. I dig in for the night. It rains all night. Thunder and lightning. Lightning hits the lightning rod at least six times, sending electrostatic electricity through the metal of the helicopter pad.

Finally, at five thirty, it stops raining. I come out of the little cubby hole to stretch my legs, and as I stand there stretching, here they come. I can hear them from far away. I look down at my watch. "Six oh three. Right on time," I say.

"Now I have to play this right," I think to myself.

Three helicopters, heavily guarded. I don't have enough bullets. The first helicopter lands. They make haste into the little room. Retinal scan, DNA scan, each person enters into the doors one by one and disappears as the doors shut behind them. I sit underneath the helicopter pad, not really being able to see too much. But the last helicopter is on the pad now, and there they go, one by one.

As a guard stands outside of the little building where the room is that takes the scans, the helicopter takes off. The guard looks into the room each time somebody goes in. As soon as he looks in the last time, he himself goes in. I make haste. As quick as I can, I run over to the side and look in. A retinal scan, a hand print scan, a DNA scan, and then he puts his thumb on this little thing, a blood type scan. "Welcome, Security Guard Number 321787641. Security Levels 1 through 100. You are to secure every other level from 89 down to 57. Approximate time, seven hours forty-five minutes."

The guard mumbles underneath his breath while the titanium doors open up, "Yeah another day, another fifty cents, helicopter in, helicopter out. I expected to be a president's guard by now, working for the CIA or the FBI, but no, I'm guarding a blankety blank building."

As soon as he steps into the titanium doors with his back to me, I run up and karate chop him right across the neck. He goes out like a light bulb. The doors shut. "Destination 89th floor. You will begin your security at hallway A102 and scan through C, D, and E corridors. After the floor is complete, retinal scan to re-enter."

"Great, I'm gonna have to cut this guy's eye out. It's a good thing I'm in a good mood today," I think as I decide to carry him around with me.

With my memory coming back, I realize the elevator is extremely slow. It is air induction. On the way up, it will suck the air out of the shaft that the elevator is in. When the elevator goes down, it has to fill up the bottom of the tube and then let air out of the tube as the elevator slowly goes down. Very ingenius actually. In between the floors in the walls of the shaft are things that clamp out and slow the elevator down to the floor it is going to stop on.

As I go down, I keep thinking. It is something Knuckles said to me. "Yeah Boss, I shot you in the head. I'm so sorry." And then it replays in my head again. "I'm sorry I shot you in the head," Knuckles kept telling me. But that ain't the way I remember it.

Old Snitch, being a thief and all and being small time, he thought he would move up in the world. So when he saw one of the gang go in a building, he just followed him right on in and not knowing that it was the big boss, he thought he would just wait until he was addressed and tell him why he was there. I wanna join the gang, he would say. That's what he thought anyway.

But when he went up the steps and went into the boss' office, well old Snitch, walked in right behind him, and the old mob boss had not even seen him, not one time, the whole time he was walking behind him. He walked over to his desk and looked over to the right at his safe.

Old Snitch, not very far behind him, watched him kneel down, thirty to the right, two turns to the left to three. and back to nineteen. Old Snitch saw behind the coffee table. Well, there was one of them foldouts that came across the floor into a divider. He slowly backed up back behind that divider.

That's when I walked in. The old boss trusted me with everything, even his life, but little did he know, today would be the day, the day that he would betray me in every way as Snitch watched us leave one after another, the old mob boss not even locking his office door as I followed him out shortly after.

"Well," old Snitch thought, "I'm a dead man," and little did he know, he was because this was one mob boss he didn't want to betray as he went over and stood in front of that safe with the door half open. He looked at the door, and then he took his foot and eased the door until it was in light view. The old pill head knelt down as skinny and bony as he was, and with his old eyes sunk down into his head, he looked at those stacks of hundreds. And then he looked at the little black bags. But that ain't what caught his eye. It was the white stuff. Three kilos.

He looked up on top of the safe. There were five green bags, just big enough to hold all the loot, the diamonds that were in the black bags, and a pound of weed with some rolling papers. He couldn't help but to think to himself that he had hit the jackpot as he stashed the money in the bags. Sweat began to pour from his brow.

He ran to the window as fast as he could and looked down into the street. "There goes the mob boss and his thug with him," he thought to himself.

He ran to the front door as fast as he could, and when he got down to the steps, he stuck the bag partially under his shirt to conceal it the best he could as he walked down the sidewalk. That's when he turned around. "Oh no, it's Knuckles! Oh, he probably won't even recognize me. He ain't very smart at all," he thought to himself as he ducked down behind a car and disappeared.

As I stand there, still waiting on the slow elevator, I remember more....

"Yeah Boss, the big boss said we had to deliver this package," Knuckles said to me. I looked down on the seat as he went on, "When you deliver it, pick up the other package and then bring it back to the boss. He's paying us one hundred grand a piece."

I looked down at the box. What could be worth so much? Or better yet, what could it be exchanged for. I questioned Knuckles. "Knuckles, I'm sure you heard the boss wrong, maybe ten thousand, and we split it down the middle each." That was usually the operation, but we did ten or fifteen jobs a day sometimes.

We reached the yard. It was another abandoned warehouse the big boss owned through a company named, well, I can't read it. The word's too long, and my education is too short. But this one was a newer warehouse. Knuckles pulled in through the fence through the open gate, and there it was, a long black Chevy van with no windows on the side or the back. He slowed down to almost a stop as he pulled straight in front of the van. Over to the right about three feet, but it put the middle of our hoods dead lined with the sides of each vehicle.

Knuckles said, "I don't like this. Maybe you oughta go around to the back and go around this way where I can keep an eye on you." He pulled out a .45 and put it in his left hand and put his arm halfway out of the window with the gun on the inside. "That way if there's any trouble, I'll be able to cover you, you know what I mean?"

"Sure, Knuckles, I know what you mean."

I grabbed the box, did exactly what Knuckles said, and went around the back. Then I came up to the driver's door and went around the front to the left side, the passenger side of the van. Still not seeing anybody, I walked on. I pulled out my .357 and pulled the hammer back. After I passed the passenger's window, I walked on back, and with the sun on the other side and not seeing any shadows, I was feeling pretty good until I got to the back and there was no one there.

I sat the box down. But little did I know it, Knuckles was over there with a remote mashing the button on it. After I opened the van door and saw Knuckles through the van's windshield as he got out of the car, I walked on around. That's when Knuckles came around the front of the van. He pointed that .45 right at my head and said, "Sorry, old friend," and pulled the trigger. There I laid, dead. Knuckles grabbed my .357, got in the car, and drove off.

The senator had heard rumors of a young man by my name. It was me. The young man that wouldn't die. At first, it was fun and games, but not to the senator. They had developed a chip that was unthinkable. He had tried it on ten men and dropped them in the middle of real war games. It was the greatest military defense weapon there was. Only one problem, the multi- billion dollar chip didn't last long because the men died quickly from wounds. But when the senator heard of Zon Zombie, of course that wasn't my name back then, he had me followed, and the unimaginable happened right before his eyes.

As he pulled up in an SUV right outside the courtyard of the old abandoned warehouse, he could hardly believe what he was seeing. As Knuckles drove out of the gate, the senator and his team pulled up to the old abandoned van. There I laid. Heart just about to stop beating. His team got out and shot a great big shot of adrenaline right in my chest.

"Quick, get him in the back of the SUV. I've got a doctor standing by right now," the senator told them.

They looked down on the ground at brain matter and skull bone and skin and hair. It had blown the whole side of my head off. The man who wouldn't die was now as dead as he could be as they took me off to the hospital.

Six long hours, and then they exchanged surgeons. Five and a half more hours, and then another surgeon came in. After ten or fifteen surgeons and three days of my skull being wide open, a plastic surgeon came in and finished the job.

"Ah, there, good as new," he said, as I laid there as a vegetable.

The senator came in, "Yes, Senator, we finished. As you can see, he looks good as new," the doctor said.

"How long before he wakes up?"

"If the chip reboots his brain, anytime now."

"Well, we better get out of here now. I don't want him to see us, especially together. Do not let him know anything about me."

He took out a small tablet, top of the line military grade computer. It could even do 3D imaging. He began to program it, and after he was through, I woke up.

Knuckles was on his way to the warehouse, at least one of them at that time. As he pulled up in front, he saw old Snitch running down the sidewalk. He had a green sack, and on the bottom left hand corner, there was a yellow dollar sign about two inches tall and an inch and a half wide. It was a skinny font, so you would have to be looking straight at it to see it, especially on that green. That's when Snitch had turned around and seen Knuckles.

Knuckles, not being too smart, thought to himself, "I know that guy, and I know where he stays, too."

After shooting me, he quickly went up to the boss. "Hey Boss, you know who I just saw? Snitch."

"Yeah, nevermind that. Did you get the job done?" That's when he called me by real name, for the last time, of course.

"Yeah Boss, the remote didn't work like you showed me. Yeah, I mashed this button here just like you said, right in the middle."

"Now Knuckles, that ain't what I said at all. I said you've got to click this switch up here to the on position and then you mash that button in the middle. How hard was that? You're an explosives expert. You like blowing up stuff."

"Yeah Boss, but this new technology..."

"What new technology, Knuckles? It's just one button."

"Yeah, I guess you're right, but anyway I got the job taken care of. He's dead. I shot him right in the head, and I'm gonna tell you, Boss, it don't feel too good. If I ever see him again, I'm gonna tell him I'm sorry."

The big boss' eyes got big. "What do you mean, see him again? You saw his brains out on the cement, didn't you?"

"Why sure I did."

"Okay then, nobody can live without a brain."

"But Boss, I've seen him..."

"What do you mean, you've seen him?"

"He's been shot, didn't even go to the hospital, stabbed, hit in the head with a crowbar. He fell down an elevator shaft while getting in a fight with one of the brawlies. He killed the other guy, but he got up and walked away."

"So you're the one been spreading that zombie crap everywhere? You got everybody scared to death."

"Boss, it's true. Why'd you want me to blow him up anyway?"

He settled down and sat back in his chair. He said, "Well, I've heard them stories, too. I didn't know it was you spreading the rumors, but I had my suspicion. But now that I know it's a bunch of nonsense, I ain't worried about it. A shot in the head's good enough, but blowing him to smithareens, he couldn't have come back from that, even if he would have been a zombie."

Now old Knuckles had forgotten about Snitch. But he didn't forget about shooting me in the head, and it was bothering him. He asked the big boss again, "Why'd you do it, Boss? I still don't feel good about it."

The boss looked at his safe again. He said, "You see that safe over there? I keep a small portion of money in it, a half a million or so, along with a small portion of diamonds, and a little weed, and a little bit of the white stuff, you know, just to keep my nose cool every now and then. Well, earlier today, I had him in here talking about a big heist, a big bank job. Of course, I was gonna get my cut for filling you guys in."

"Hey Boss, how come you didn't tell me nothing about the bank heist?"

"Shut up, Knuckles, and listen. I went out the door shortly after, and he went out after me. Then we left the building together. When I came back into my office and looked in my safe, one of my green bags was gone and everything in my safe." He held up a green bag with a little dollar sign emblem on the bottom left corner.

"Hey Boss, I saw that same bag in Snitch's hand."

The mob boss' eyes got really big and really glassy. "Knuckles, are you sure? This ain't good, you know that right?"

"What do you mean, Boss?"

Knuckles finally put two and two together. "I killed one of my best men, and he didn't steal my loot. Your little friend the Snitch did," the boss said.

"Boss, that's what Snitch does. He's a thief, and he snitches on everybody else."

"Knuckles, go get my loot. Take one finger at a time, starting with the toes, and don't stop 'til you get to the end of the fingers. If he ain't talked by then, you take rubber bands and put 'em around the stubless feet so it'll stop the bleeding."

"But Boss, don't you want him to die quickly?"

"Yes, but not too quick. There was over a million dollars worth of diamonds in that loot. Recover my diamonds. Anything else you recover is yours."

"Okay, Boss."

"And listen, I don't believe that bull about him being zombie, being able to come back to life or not being able to die." That's when he looked down to the ground and said, "But just in case, you better make up some kind of story. I'll go along with whatever you think of."

As I snap out of it, I think, "Man, this elevator is really slow." I go back to remembering. I hadn't known what had really happened, of course, but I had figured it out as I went, putting pieces together from what I heard here and there.

Now old Knuckles wasn't very smart, as I've said before. But thinking that he had killed me and all, well it didn't sit too good with him, and now he had put two and two together. It took him a while as he entered into Snitch's lair, thinking that he would put the rubber bands on first to make sure Snitch didn't die too quick at all because the way he felt was painful and he didn't like it at all.

It was several months before. Knuckles had a run in with a dirty cop, and when he took him down, he took his cop Taser with him, so when he entered into the lair where Snitch was, he pointed that old Taser right at his throat, pulled the trigger, and held it down. Old Snitch stood there for a second, and then his feet flopped out from under him as he hit the floor, shaking from head to toe.

149

Knuckles let off the trigger and looked at the Taser. "Wow, I like this thing!" he thought. Then he pulled the trigger again. Old Snitch bounced up and down off the ground. He was drooling out of the mouth. Knuckles pulled the trigger back and the retractor and jerked it out of his throat. He burned him good. Snitch laid there dazed and confused.

Knuckles went in and grabbed a glass of water out of the not so clean dishes that were in the sink, dumped it in his face, and then knelt down in front of him. "I'm gonna ask you one time. Where's the green bag with the loot?"

Still dazed and confused, Snitch shook his head no as if he didn't know. Knuckles took out some tie wraps, set him up in a chair, and tied his arms to the arm rest of the chair and his legs to the legs of the chair. Then he pulled out a two by four from inside of his coat and put it underneath his feet where his toes hung over. Then he pulled out two great big rubber bands, folded them three times, put them up on his foot, and then took another tie wrap and wrapped his foot down to the two by four.

Still dazed and confused with a little blood dripping out of his nose, Snitch watched old Knuckles drag out those big clippers, the curved kind, the plant clippers. Knuckles said, "Oh yeah, I almost forgot." Then he got a rag and stuck it in Snitch's mouth, wrapped a bandana around his mouth, and tied it in the back of his head. "That ain't so you won't yell," Knuckles said. "That's so that you won't hurt my ears when you do yell."

And that's just what Snitch did as Knuckles clipped one toe after another one. As the tears rolled out of his eyes and the veins swelled up on his neck, still only a few drops of blood, and when he got to the last toe on the other foot, Snitch blacked out.

Knuckles went back to the sink and grabbed another cup of water. He took the rag out of Snitch's mouth. Knuckles said it one more time, "Where's the loot, and I won't ask you again. I'm gonna kill you either way it goes. I just want you to know that. I've never lied about that, and I'm gonna kill you slow either way it goes, whether I get the money or not."

"I'll tell you," Snitch said, "but please kill me first."

"If I kill you first," Knuckles said, "how are you going to tell me where the money is? You want to write it down on a piece of paper?"

"If you promise to kill me quick, I'll tell you"

Knuckles thought about it for a second, and then he said, "Okay."

"It's over there in the coffee table."

Knuckles retrieved the money, almost all of it. Old Snitch was too busy smoking the weed and doing the drugs to care anything about money or a couple of stones he didn't know what to do with, being a small time thief as he was. After Snitch saw a big smile come up on Knuckles' face, he could imagine what he was thinking.

He cried out, "Now shoot me in the head! I can't stand the pain!"

Knuckles grabbed the rag. Snitch cried out, "You said you would kill me quick!"

"Oh, I lied."

"But you said while ago that you wouldn't tell me a lie."

"And I didn't, up to that point. I didn't lie when I said I was

151

going to kill you and I was going to do it slowly and it didn't matter whether you gave me the money or not. Negotiation was over after that."

Snitch couldn't help but to think how smart Knuckles was, but retrieving that money gave him the esteem of a college education, knowing that when he got back with the loot how happy the boss was going to be. He finished the job alright. Snitch made it to eight fingers before he passed away, but the word got around quick as I was trying to make heads or tails of who I was and why I woke up in a hospital with a big ol' scar on my head.

When I finally step off the elevator, the titanium doors open again. I am confused at first as I drag the guard off onto the floor with me. But then I look down on the floor of the elevator. His badge had fallen off. Apparently, it had a reader in it, and whatever kind of security it was, it was reading that he was still on the elevator. So I quickly retrieve the badge and think, "Well, I'll just use this badge to make my rounds."

But at the end of the hall, I see a dark figure, at least I think I do. I go to the first room. Then I think I hear voices. I drag the guard in quickly. Then I sit him in a chair, a nice comfortable one. I prop his head up to look like he is sleeping. "My, my, you're a lazy one today," I think to myself as I say it out loud, "Make sure you don't get caught sleeping on the job. I don't think your boss would like that."

I walk around for thirty minutes or so, eager to find what I am looking for, but there is nothing. Each guard was assigned to different floors, and I knew this one was assigned to thirty or so and I had seven hours and forty-five minutes to find what I was looking for. Now with forty-five minutes gone, time is running out.

After I get the guard good and cozy, I head out the door. I carry the badge with me. The little red light on the door, I hadn't noticed, but above each name plate was a little LED light, and when the badge was recognized, the door would automatically unlock. So all I have to do is push it open. There are no doorknobs. As soon as I walk up to a door, I push it open, look in, table, chairs, nothing of use, nothing of value. Not even a computer terminal. The whole floor, nothing.

By the time I get to the D corridor, there is another elevator. I quickly make haste back to the other elevator on A corridor. I go and grab the guard and drag him out. The doors won't open. Then I remember the elevator saying to scan corridors A through E. I grab him by the back of the shirt and start dragging him down the hallway. Then I think to myself, "The hell with this."

I go and grab a chair out of the room. It has wheels on it. I throw him in the chair. "Ah, that's much easier," I say to myself as I push him down the hallway. Finally I get to the E corridor. There is nothing but titanium doors. No buttons to mash.

"You are running late," it says as the big doors open. "You are exactly three minutes behind schedule, Security Guard such and such number. Voice recognition failure."

"That's not good," I think to myself. I smack him on the face, not too gentle.

As soon as he wakes up, he says, "What?"

"Voice recognition accepted. 87th floor," it says as the big doors shut.

His eyes are wide open. "What's going on?"

I am going to need this guy to get down through the floors, but I have a feeling it is going to take seven hours. Each floor has an elevator that goes two floors down while acting like it only goes one. I didn't know that at the time, but there were secret floors. But how did they get to them? From eighty-nine to fifty-seven, you have to go in one corridor, down the floor, and out another way through another corridor. It is just a giant maze. "A stairway would be nice. Surely they have some kind of fire escape." I think all this as I think about what to do with the guard. He is still dazed and confused, but he is scared to death.

After I push the chair out of the elevator, he doesn't move. I say, "Tell me what you know."

"And if I don't?"

"I'll snap your neck like a pretzel."

He begins to tremble. "Listen, Mister, all I do is walk these halls every day. I've been doing it for eight months. I'm sick to death of it. It's just an empty building."

"What do you mean, it's an empty building? Why so much security? Where do the people go when they go in these rooms?"

"I don't know. I've never been allowed to go into the rooms. Unless we're called in there, we're not allowed in any of the facilities. Each person has an assigned destination in the building, maybe a lab or a computer room. I don't know. But you'll never get in. It isn't like the rooms that we search and make sure are empty and secure. It's more like, well, it's more secure than a military prison. The roof elevator, each time it comes up, it comes up for a different elevator."

"What do you mean?"

"I mean, when the elevator goes down, it takes that person to a particular part in the building, and then another one comes back up. Like the elevator I'm on, it's just for me and these floors. When I come back up, I have to come up the same way, through all these mazes."

"You do this every day?"

"Yeah, every day, seven hours, forty-five minutes, such and such guard with number such and such. You're two minutes late. You're one minute early. You have to wait for the elevator. All day, every day, seven hours of listening to this machine. You're five minutes late. Your break is over. It's time to take a break. Your heart rate is too fast. You'll have to walk a little slower the next round or vice versa. Sometimes I wish I had a boss that would just curse me out all day, do this, do that, but no. I've taken one day off."

"What'd you do on your day off"

"Are you kidding? I'm on a military installation when I get off here. The helicopter takes us back to a base. None of us are allowed to leave. They contract us for a year. We get twenty-five dollars an hour. After the end of the year, we get six figures, but everybody has to do a year's work, and my day off, it wasn't a day off. I was sick as a dog."

"What about the military implants?"

His eyes get big. "What military implants?"

That's when he looks at the scar on my head. I know he knows something. By this time, his nerves have settled down, and the fear has left him. He rubs his neck and his shoulder. "You really gave me a good wallop...." His lips begin to cross the words, and slobber begins to drip down his lips onto his shirt.

"Go on, finish what you were saying."

"I've only heard rumors of the military chips."

"What's wrong with you?"

He begins to mumble as if he is talking, and then he just dies.

"Well, this ain't good. I must have hit him really hard. Somehow I gave him brain damage and killed him. I've never done that before," I think to myself. "Yeah, right. But I'm an expert at it." Then I get to thinking, "Well, maybe not."

Without that voice recognition and the heartbeat, I am going to have trouble. DNA scan, blood type scan, retinal scan. I have to make it back to the top of the building, and I know it. But I get to thinking about his death. The hit couldn't have possibly killed him. But he died with his eyes opened, and when I go to pick him up, it is his left eye. It is wide open, but his eye is sunken in just a little bit inside the eyeball. I turn his head to the side and look into his ear just a little bit. It is thick red goo inside of it. No doubt, a small explosion, just enough to kill him and not enough to notice on the outside unless you were very observant.

If only I was in the old buildings. I have to think quick. No fire escape. No fire extinguisher. No fire hose, not even hydrants in the ceiling to put fires out. If I get on the elevator, it's going to take me a floor down, farther away from the roof. That's even if I can manage to get it to work for me, which is highly improbable.

I look at the end of the hall. It's just a wall. I open the doors to each room. No outside windows. Down each corridor I go. Finally, a window. It is four inches thick, six feet tall, and six inches wide. Great. I'm in prison, like a rat in a maze. I pound on some of the walls. It isn't sheetrock. It is thick hard wood. There is no breaking through it. Whoever built this place meant business, but why so much security?

That's when I get to thinking. The guard's heart stopped. Surely they have a protection mode. I go back to the elevators and drag the chair around back to the A section on this floor which will go down to another floor, but this time, I have an idea. I put the badge back on the guard and stand him before the elevator. The doors open up. I push him on in.

"Voice recognition."

I make a grunting sound and push him off in the floor, and then I push the chair out of the elevator.

"Code seven, emergency procedure."

I feel the floor move. It makes haste upward. Somewhere in the ninetieth floors, it stops. I get over to the side of the doors. When they open, two guards come in and grab the injured guard. The one with his back toward me kinda hides me from the other one. But as soon as he pulls the body out, he exposes me to the one guard that now sees me.

All hell breaks loose. "Intruder," he cries. That's when I step through the big doors.

"Red alert," the elevator speaker says, and as he is coming out of the door, the other one is going for his Taser and so is he. Right before the doors shut, I jump through. The other guard tries to come through, too. The doors get him. Pinched him like a piece of toast.

"Intruder alert, intruder alert."

157

Now this hallway is different. On both sides, it is solid glass all the way down with glass doors entering into glass rooms. By the time I get a glimpse of all this, I have already been shot and tasered. I stand there shaking with little effect. I look down at the Tasers that are sticking out of my ribs. I grab the lit up wires and jerk them out, prongs too.

The guard looks at me. I take the palm of my hand and push him in the chest real hard and real fast. He goes up against the glass. I think it is hard enough to push him through it, but no, he hits his head up against the hard glass. It is way too thick to bust.

"Intruder alert."

By that time, everybody is looking through the glass at me. There are four scientists, and each glass room has one scientist in it. On one side of the hall, there are two great big rooms with two scientists on that side and the same on the other side.

I go to the first room. There are all kinds of lab stuff, microscopes, beakers, glass tubes that go around in a circle from the ceiling down to the table with stuff dripping out of it.

The scientist says, "How did you get in? You can't come through those doors. Nobody can."

"What do you mean?" I ask.

Those glass doors go down from the ceiling down to the floor, but above in the ceiling, there are square plates. Only military supervision can go through those doors. I hadn't recognized it until I went through, but the red alert had went off.

A voice comes over the speaker. "Military adviser, awaiting further instructions."

"Oh, I'm sorry, sir. You didn't look...well, you didn't look like...," the scientists says.

"Well, I didn't look like what?"

"You didn't look like military, sir."

I look down at myself. Then I realize it is the chip in my head. Something activated it, but what and how? I say, "Listen, there is a chip in my head."

"Of course there is. You're a militant serbo."

"A what?"

"Yeah, that's how you got in here. You've got the new chip, right?"

"Yeah, that's right. Keep on talking. I kinda lost my memory. Can you help me out a little bit?"

"Sure, but how did you get in here?"

"I don't really remember," I say, lying of course, playing dumb. I've gotten pretty good at it over the years. I've learned if you play dumb in the right areas and right situations that people like to prove their smartness. It's gotten me out of a bunch of jams in the past. But this scientist is too smart, you know the type, which is going to prove to be his ignorance.

He fills me in on everything. Each room on each floor designs a particular part in programming. The government is using cybernetics on would be dead men, such as myself. When there is no brain activity, they will give them a supercharged chip. But mine is more advanced, and that's what this building was all about, building the chip along with the power to run it and all of its components.

With me already having a reputation of being a terror, the government had eyes on me more way before this, way before the gun shot wound. Little did I know that my survival skills were phenomenal. It had caught a lot of attention, along with the rumors. But now with a gun shot to the head and brain dead, they had nothing to lose, along with ten others just like me. They call them super serbo insurgeons.

"So what happened to me?" I ask. He tells me everything from a to z. I ask him, "Why are you giving me all this information?"

"Well, it's pretty obvious," he says. "Anybody that has the clearance to come into this room, all this knowledge that I'm giving you has the same clearance that I have or above. So I'm not breaking protocol, and no one that is not supposed to be in this room can get in this room. That includes you. You would've never been able to step in the elevators."

I get to thinking. Why didn't the elevators see me? Why didn't they stop me? And the doors to the rooms that I searched, each one of them. I thought it was the badge, but I didn't have the badge when I entered into this one.

That's when a gas comes out of the ceiling, lithium nitrate with ammonium sulfite, along with other acetone gasses. I watch the scientist began to melt down. First, his hair falls off onto his shoulders. "Well, this ain't good," I think to myself.

Ten guards run down the glass hall while the scientist is holding my attention. One at a time, they come down the elevator until there are ten of them. They crouch down outside of the room with automatic weapons aimed toward me. "The hallway is secure."

Then the elevator doors open up again, but this time, I am

160

aware of what is going on. A highly decorated soldier comes through. By this time, things are melting around me, and I notice the hairs on my arm are gone. I touch my other arm. It is the acetone. It is all over the room. He stands there looking at me through the glass wall. Then he looks at his watch. The scientist is dead on the floor.

"Military mode activated." I head toward the big glass doors.

10

When I wake up, I am on the roof, and the soldier, if that's what he is, lays dead behind me as I wait on the helicopter. But what happened? How did I get here?

I drag the soldier underneath the helicopter pad and wait patiently. Here it comes. After seven long hours. As soon as it lands, the elevator doors begin to open. A scientist comes out. As they go up the steps to the helicopter pad. I step in right behind him. He doesn't see me, and he can't hear me because of the helicopter. The pilot sees me walking behind him and figures I came up with him, I guess.

But as soon as I get on the helicopter, the scientist says, "Where did you come from? I didn't see you in here when I left."

"I'm here to help," I say.

"Well, that isn't protocol. And where are the guards at?"

I take my fist and pound it into his face. I say, "There's the guard."

The copilot turns around and sees what I have done. By that time, here comes another scientist. I take my gun and hit the co-pilot in the head. I say, "Take off right now."

The pilot starts lifting the helicopter up. The other scientist grabs a hold of the sled that the helicopter landed on. After about twenty feet up, he can't hang on any longer. I think, "What the heck. I'll grab him and pull him in." When I do, I just about get a hold of his hands before he lets go.

That's when the pilot turns to the side and tries to dump me out of the door. It almost works. I grab the handle to the door. As the helicopter goes sideways, it also goes forward. But then it levels back out, and I am able to get back in, still with my gun in my hand.

I say, "You try that again, you'll be dead."

"Who is going to fly the helicopter if I'm dead?"

"I will."

When I say that, he snaps right out it. "Now take me back to the base," I tell him.

"Mister, I can't do that."

I shoot a hole in the seat right between his legs. He says, "You can kill me if you want to, but there is no way I'm going to give you the location of that base."

I look up at the automatic pilot. As soon as he sees my eyes see it, he looks up, too. He looks back at me, and I look back at him. He knows I have no need for him then. He goes to grab for the automatic pilot, to sabotage it, no doubt, but that thick helmet he has is no match for my bullet as it goes through the helmet and out the other side. The helmet flies apart into three big pieces as the bullet goes out the side through the glass.

I click on automatic pilot, then I sit back and enjoy the ride. We fly over some desert. It is hot terrain and dry. But after an hour of flying, I finally see a tower up ahead and then another one. I shut the side doors, and that's when I see it coming, up between the two towers up far away. First, it looks like a drawing canvas. Two light streams coming straight up and then coming straight toward me. Missiles.

Buzzers start blinking off and on. "Military evasive." Automatic pilot kicks in for defense, and then all the sudden, it just goes off. The helicopter hovers there, but here come those missiles straight for me. I throw a rope out of the side door, and as quick as I can, I jump out. Thirty feet of rope. I hang on. And when I get to the end of it, it snatches me and swings me back around. I let go of another ten feet and hang on as it swings me back the other way. And still fifty feet or so off the ground, when it slings me back the other way, I let go, so it swings me well out of the way.

As soon as I hit the ground and roll, I begin to run. I feel the heat of it on my neck and shoulders. Right where I am running, a ten feet piece of the helicopter blade sticks in the ground right before me. I stop cold in my tracks. As I look up behind me, pieces blow in every direction. I quickly get behind the blade with what little protection it gives as the fiery furnace falls out of the sky onto the ground.

Here come two military trucks. "Military mode activated."

Everything goes black.

When I wake up, I am on the military base. There is blood seeping out of holes, but I don't know how they got there. But this time, there is a senator.

"Why are you still alive?" I ask him.

He says, "Because you can't kill me."

"Why is that?"

"It's simple. That military hardware you have, it belongs to me. You will kill anything around me, but you can't hurt me."

He takes out a gun and points it to his head as if he is going to shoot himself. Everything goes black. When I come to, I have the gun in my hand.

"See, you can't even let me kill myself," the senator says.

I look down, wondering how I got his gun. I was ten feet away from him. "How did you program me, and why can't I remember what I'm doing?"

"I find it much easier when a soldier does what he's told and has no memory of it. That's why I choose brain dead people."

"I don't understand. What does brain dead have to do with it?"

"Well, that's what helps you forget when you come out of military mode. See, we didn't repair your brain. But with your special gifts, you have become our number one priority for the last ten years."

"What do you mean?"

"Organized crime."

"I don't understand."

"Well, you're the one that's organizing it."

It is all beginning to make sense. He has been using me to

take out the mob bosses and turn them against each other. All the long while, military shipments were going out to different countries. Missiles to Iran. Automatic weapons to Iraq. Nuclear bombs to North Korea.

But the one thing he didn't count on was that with my re-generation of healing, my brain was healing, too. I begin to remember the doctor's office and a few other times that military mode kicked in. My brain is healing. And the chip is integrated with my new memories.

"But the programming of the chip? Who programmed the chip?" I ask.

"Well, I did.'"

"And how did you do that?"

"Well, it's simple." He lifts up a pad. "All the programming is right here on this pad, encrypted. Not even you can break into this pad."

But I know I can't hurt him, and I can't let him hurt himself. "So nobody can overwrite the programming. Is that what you're saying?"

"Yes, exactly."

"So basically, I'm just your robot."

"Exactly, even if you did try to overwrite it, you can't change the program."

"But I'm here."

"Only because I summoned you here. You see the military post in town that you've been playing around in, it was all to see how far you could get. That was a top security place, more secure than this base, and nobody knows where this base is. You see those towers? There are jamming signals, magnetic propulsion, not even sonar can see this place. No satellite, nothing."

"So pretty much, nobody knows we are here, right?"

"That's right, just you and me."

"What about the rest of the soldiers?"

"Look, Zon, when you went into military mode, you killed everybody on this base."

"How many was that?"

"There were over three hundred guards on this base."

I look down. That explains everything, why I'm bleeding.

"You're my number one prize, Zon Zombie. This was the ultimate test."

"So you killed hundreds of people just so you could test out a theory, whether I would live or die doing it?"

"Along with the hundreds you've killed before this. Remember, you're a killer, and the underground terror you've been fighting against..." That's when he looks at me with a cold sobering voice and says, "You're the terror."

It runs through me like cold ice as I remember the letter. "To the terror," the envelope said. I can hardly believe it as I remember opening it and reading the letter addressed to me.

But that doesn't explain why I am alive. And why the bullet holes are healing as I stand here. I've got to get rid of this tablet. A programmer. But I can't get ten feet close to him.

He holds up the tablet and says, "I think its time for you to go back to what you were doing."

"What is that exactly?"

"Organizing all the crime. See, once you're in control..... But

I'm in control of you. I get all the money, all the goods. I get everything."

"I guess you want me to take the big boss out," I say.

"I am the big boss," he says. That's when I realize, the voice, the eyes. He is right. He has played me the whole time.

"And who is this other boss the girl works for?"

"Oh, that's Colonel so and so. I have no further use for him. You will be killing him when you get back."

"No, I won't. I'm through killing. At least for you, I am."

He laughs me to scorn. I begin to laugh with him. Then he looks at me. "What are you laughing at?" he asks.

"I can remember what I've done."

"That's impossible. Your brain was scattered all over your head. It's a wonder the chip even worked at all. Your doctor, he was a master surgeon. I almost hated to kill him."

"So it's you that's been doing all the killing all along?"

"Why, of course."

"With people like you in the government, America doesn't stand a chance."

"America? I'm not after America."

Then I get to thinking, "No, he's after the world."

"I'm doing the same thing with the countries as you did with the mob bosses. It's the same game. Supply North Korea with nuclear arms and keep inner disturbance throughout the other small countries, automatic weapons, turmoil, small explosives, and not to mention the pill heads and drug addicts. I'll have control of the drugs, the cartels. Me and you are partners. For...as long as one of us lives."

168

"What do you mean?"

"You see, you'll carry on, even after I die."

"I remember what I've done in military mode. Like I said before, my brain is healing."

"Oh yeah, well tell me what you did the time you went into military mode at the building when you woke up on the top floor."

"How did you know that?"

"It's right here on this keypad. I see what you see, and I know you couldn't have seen what you did after you woke up on the top floor. Or even what you did on this base."

The fact is I can't remember. But I do remember the doctor's house now. But it was a long time ago, and it seems like the further away it is, the more I remember about it. But I saw what happened at the doctor's house, so I wasn't going to be convincing. But I know my brain is healing. I'm at a dead end.

The senator says, "It's time for you to sleep," as he mashes down on the keypad with his finger.

It was hot. There was fire all around. The helicopter was a blazing. There was rich black smoke up in the sky. First, it was a military SUV that pulled up beside me. The first one out began to shoot. It was slow motion, a bullet coming straight at my eye. It was almost as if I could reach up and touch it as I pulled my head back and watched it go by.

Then here came another one. But before I could even aim my gun, I had already shot it, and the bullet went straight into the soldier that climbed out of the SUV. Then another shot went off as another one climbed out, and then a third, and then a fourth.

All four of them in the left eye. They dropped where they stood. The action on my gun stayed open. I was out of bullets.

I quickly apprehended two guns from the deceased as the other SUV pulled up beside it, and four more soldiers got out. By this time, the truck was already upon us. As I ran toward the SUV, they dropped like flies as I jumped over across the hood. That's when I felt the sting in my belly. A half of a dozen men got out of the back of the truck. Automatic weapons. They let it rip. It was all in slow motion.

I took the gun as the bullets came toward me slowly, and I took the barrel and hit each bullet downward. As I got to the last bullet, I sent bullets sailing back. Twelve soldiers died. Each in the left eye. But the last one, it was a little off. "Correction," some kind of computer registered inside of my eye. "Point oh one three degree correction." By this time, the other truck had already emptied out its soldiers and began to fire. Thirty men laid dead within twenty seconds.

I climbed in the SUV and headed for the gates. One hundred ten, one hundred twenty, one hundred thirty, one hundred forty miles per hour. The dust was about to raise the back end off the ground when I hit the great big gates. The bottom of the gates folded under and pulled the top down to the ground. When the front end hit the top guidelines, it stopped the SUV cold in its tracks right there at the gate.

The airbag came in. It smushed the door to where it wouldn't open. The windshield was completely gone. My legs were pinned tightly underneath. The guardhouse was hooked to the gate. It jerked the guardhouse four feet off its foundation, killing the guard inside and wounding the other one that was on the outside real bad.

With my leg stuck, I pushed as hard as I could on the steering wheel with my back up against the seat. With incredible force, the dash began to move forward and the seat began to move backward. By then, guards were all over the place. Bullets were just a flying. The seat unbuckled from the floor board from the force as I pushed back. Into the back seat I went. Over the back seat I went, and out the back door as it raised up.

I stood to my feet and walked toward the gate. One to the right. Two to the left. And ten to the left of them. Five to the left of me. And one to the left of that farther back.

Immediate danger. The first one shot right in the eye, the closest one to me, along with the four beside him almost at the same time. As they fell, the one on the right side held up his automatic weapon, and almost simultaneously, I dropped six more. The gun was emptied by then. I held up the other one and emptied it out as soldiers fell to the ground.

As I walked over the front, over the hood, over the gate and the mangled up metal, I picked up an automatic rifle. Here came a dozen more running around. I pulled the trigger and each bullet hit in the left eye of every soldier. As fast as an automatic weapon could shoot, they fell dead, one after another one, not even getting a shot off.

That's when my shoulder began to sting as I picked up another automatic weapon, and as fast as I could throw them down, soldiers fell to the ground, not missing a shot. I went through the base picking up automatic weapons that weren't even fired after the soldiers laid dead beside them. After over thirty minutes of warfare, three hundred laid dead. Thirty-five horrible minutes of blood shed and blood splatter.

Last one standing. I tried to raise up my gun to shoot him. "Exit military mode." Then, I ended up in front of the senator.

After remembering all this, I wake up back in town, back in an old building. My apartment. Was all this a dream? I look down as the wounds are healing. The last words I remember, organized crime. A government official gone bad. But I remember the notepad, the little computer that controls me, but little do I know that the senator had a chip placed in his brain, so any programming that he needed done, he did it remotely by thinking it, programming the pad, which programmed me.

But I have an advantage. Although I can't kill him, he can die. As for me, I'm not too sure I'm not already dead. The one thing I know for sure that the senator doesn't know is that these buildings will protect me. Buy why only these buildings? I have questions, and I need answers. And the answers I am getting are not helping me at all. Matter of fact, I am feeling worse now, knowing that I am a robot for a psycho senator that wants to take over the world and is well on the way.

The girl. My mob boss, my new mob boss. He is the key. Although he was militant at one time, the easy life has made him soft and fat. I go to her house. She can tell I'm in trouble. A bloody shirt. Bloody pants. I was in a hurry. No time to clean up.

I take a piece of paper and a pencil, and then I take another piece of paper and put it on top. As I write a sentence down, I cover the sentence with the other piece of paper until I get to the end. Then I write on the top piece of paper, "Read this," and then I leave.

I come back two hours later. The fat man is there. "You know the scoop?" I ask him.

"Yeah, I know the scoop. Why should I care? I'm a rich man. I've got everything I ever wanted, women, drugs, guns, money, power."

"There's only one thing you didn't think about." I pull out a gun and shoot right beside his head. "You're not protected. The senator is."

I know the senator is listening and watching everything being done, right through my own eyes. The fat man gets scared. He knows I am right. With him out of the way, the senator can't be stopped.

That's when I see it in my eye, "Military Mode Activated. Kill Colonel such and such."

I stand to my feet and walk over to the colonel. The computer writes on my eye again, "Snap the colonel's neck."

Then, the computer comes over my eye, "No immediate danger. Exit military mode." Then, "Military mode activated." Then, "Exit military mode."

Although the senator is miles away, he can't get me to kill the colonel because he doesn't have a gun. After banging on the keypad several times trying to get me to kill the colonel, I finally get a hold of the military mode. "Exit military mode."

For the first time, I have controlled it. But I am real angry. Only when I'm angry can I control it. So I get mad. I think about my friend at the warehouse. I think about all those I have killed.

Although most of them deserved it, they didn't by my hand, a just way, through the court system. And then the guard. And then the three hundred soldiers.

The senator is upset. That's when the unthinkable happens. "Military mode activate. Kill Zon Zombie. Kill colonel such and such. Along with the girl, and anybody else that stands in the way."

I maintain my civil mode, my civil stature, and my own attitude, not knowing what to do or what to say to the colonel. But he knows he is in danger. I put a blindfold on my eyes and sit down on the couch. I say, "Colonel, you will know what to do when the time comes, but I can't hurt the senator."

At least I think that, until three hours later when the door is kicked in. The first one the senator gets to is the girl. I hate to hear what I hear as I sit there with a blindfold on my eyes. College education, all that hard work, and for what? For me to bring death right to her door.

"Military mode activated. Exit military mode." It's getting hard. The military mode keeps trying to kick in.

The fat man shoots off the gun that I had laid on the coffee table prior to sitting down with the blindfold on, but the senator shoots him in the eye. He sits there dead. My plan has fallen through. The only way I was going to kill the senator was through the colonel's hand who was nothing more than a fat mob boss doing the senator's aiding and abetting and getting rich while he did it. But now, everybody lays dead underneath the senator.

The senator says, "I don't have any further use for you. Self terminate."

174

That's when I pick up the gun from the colonel's hand, and trying to pull my hand away, the gun points toward my head. I have no control over it.

"Exit military mode," I say to myself. "Exit military mode."

The double action .45, the hammer as I squeeze on the trigger begins to come back. "This is it," I think to myself, "I won't take another shot in my head."

The senator knows that, too, but anything's better than what waits for me ahead. That's when I feel the fire go inside of my head and out the other side, and I fall to the floor. But only this time, I am on my turf. My neighborhood. My turf. My buildings.

Epilogue

I was only thirteen, but I grew up in these old buildings as I stood on this rooftop as I did so many times day after day. But today was different. Local gangs figured out the roofs were the safest place to stay out of view from the cops and the mob gangs who were older and more vicious. It wasn't too long after standing there when it began to rain, not just a little bit. It came down hard.

It was an old air conditioner, the water cooler type. Three feet off the ground, it had a level of grade work done for the air conditioner to sit on, and then on the roof, the other components sat around the grading. But right underneath that grating, if you got directly under it, underneath the water cooler was completely dry and so was the water pan that was beneath it. Since the water cooler was a little wider than the pan, the pan couldn't fill up, and there was just enough room for me to climb up in there. Well, it was too low to stand. But I could lay down real good, and there I went. As soon as I got up in there, I fell asleep.

Man, I loved these old buildings. I loved the hard wood floors, the solid walls, the two inch thick doors, not like that new stuff, plastic and sheet rock. I watched them demo one building right at the edge of town one time. I couldn't help but to stand there as it crumbled to the ground. Tears filled my eyes, and they dropped onto the floor of the roof that I was standing on. Little did I know it, but my tears were absorbed and disappeared into the roof work. Every tear that hit, it was like a heart beat in my chest and it pounded through the whole city like electrostatic.

While I laid there thinking about this, a tear came out of my eyes and hit that splash pan. I felt that heartbeat again. But just as I felt the heartbeat, kaboomp, kaboomp, two tears, the door busted open, and I could see between the components of the air conditioner. It was one of the local gangs. I was scared to death at first.

I propped myself up on my arm, and here they came. There must have been eleven or twelve of them. They had some guy with 'em that they were holding. A bunch of them gathered up crates that were around the water cooler. They beat him to a pulp and threw him on those crates.

One of them said, "Look at the black stuff coming out of the pipe over there in the corner. That's tar. That stuff's flammable. Once you get it lit, nothing puts it out." Now after they threw that guy on them crates, one of them went over there and got some of that tar on a piece of cardboard, and with that cardboard soaked with that tar, or the black stuff, they threw that piece of cardboard right over the top of his body and lit the cardboard.

Now they watched that cardboard light up, and so did I. At first, it didn't look like the tar was going to burn. But then it started fizzing and sparking, and once it started doing that, the whole top of that cardboard was on fire on top of the guy they had on the crates. That tar was hot, and it just got hotter as it lit up. Then it melted over off the cardboard onto his body. When he woke up, he was on fire from head to toe.

I couldn't help but to make a loud sound. It haunted me when he came up screaming off of those crates. Now with his legs not able to touch the ground and his back on top of that crate, he took one breath and then laid back down as he passed out in pain.

That's when one of the gang members reached up in there where I was at and dragged me by my leg. "Take a look at this, guys."

I was screaming no and kicking. Another one grabbed my other leg. Out on the roof they got me. One held my arm. The other one held my other arm, the same with my legs, and a big guy behind me held my neck and shoulders while he squeezed real hard. The pain was intolerable.

The one on the right loosened up from my arm, and I jerked my arm backward. My elbow hit the one in back of me right in the stomach. They all let go.

"Hey, Cave Man, he hit you in the stomach. What are you gonna do about it?"

"I think I'm gonna throw him down the stairwell. Grab him!"

"No!" I said "Let me go! I won't tell anybody!"

"Oh, we're gonna make sure of that," one of them said.

I looked over at the crates. They were on fire. The smoke was going up high. Surely somebody had seen it. Maybe the cops would come. I screamed out for help. One of them grabbed my mouth and grabbed my nose and held it. I was almost to the point of blacking out. I didn't get a chance to breathe in. There was no oxygen in my lungs.

They went through the door of the rooftop into the stairway. Now it went around and around. I guess it was about eight feet across from banister to banister going down into a circle as the stairs went down floor to floor. But at the bottom where the banisters started, the top of the banister was gone but the pegs that held the banister up were still there.

The big one gave me a good wallop right in the stomach. Everything went black. I breathed out every bit of the air that I sucked in after the other one let my mouth go. My heart was pounding out of my chest, and now I couldn't breathe because I couldn't suck in air for the pain of my stomach. And with one good throw, the one they called Cave Man, the leader of the pack, he grabbed my torso and threw me over the banisters.

It was slow motion. I watched each one of them's eyes as they watched me go down. I looked down, and in slow motion, I went right on top of those pegs, the banister pegs. The slants went right through me, three of them. Two in my stomach. One right through my ribs, coming out through the right side. There was a piece of pipe also that came up out of the step of the stairway, a vent, a shaft, who knows. It stabbed me right in the back.

I laid there as I stared off as the rest of my body hit and came to a dead stop. I hung there, and I watched them come down the steps as I was in shock. One by one, they passed me.

"Don't worry. The evidence will burn up," Cave Man said, "along with the bodies. Let that be a lesson for all of ya. Anybody that crosses me, it's curtains for you, curtains." They all laughed, curtains. Cave man laughed, too, as they exited the building.

I laid there as my heart beat fainted away. My tears fell down onto the step, and it was as if the building had swollen up in anger. It was as if the windows were looking at the gang as they went up the road. The building was angry. It's mouth being the door and the windows being the eyes on the second floor. It was my imagination, of course. Or was it?

The pipe was cut at an angle, making it sharp, and half of the sharp end stuck up out of my belly. But when my tears hit the steps and absorbed into the building, the heart beat went through the city again, static electricity. It was almost ghostly.

That's when I saw it. Although I couldn't see it with my eyes, it was like I was standing over my body. The black stuff oozed through the pipe that stuck through me and the part that was in my belly, the black stuff filled me up. As my belly swelled up, the fire got worse and worse as it consumed the rooftop and now was too weak to hold anything up, including the shack that stood over the stairwell on top of the roof. The door and all came loose. Flames and all came down right on top of me.

That's when it had all really started. I woke up two buildings down. It was dark. I was in shock. I was cold. I looked down at my stomach. I couldn't believe my eyes. How was I even alive? My shirt was burnt off. My pants were burnt off. Just enough was left to cover my privates, my back side, and part of the way down on the left leg. My skin was black and charred looking. I had three or four great big holes in my stomach and my lower chest on the right side. The black stuff oozed out all over me. I held up my hands. My fingers were black and charred. When I made a fist, the skin just crumbled into ashes as it fell down onto the roof.

"I'm dead. Oh, my God! I'm dead." I looked at my hand again where the skin was that wasn't burnt. It was just a little bit between my thumb and my hand where I held my thumb together. When I spread it open and looked at the skin that wasn't charred, the skin began to grow. A little at first. It covered my thumb as the thumbnail began to grow back. It had already begun on my other arm and my hand. I just hadn't realized it yet.

But I felt full. It was a horrible full. But full of what? It was coming up my throat. It was swelling my belly up. I sat up as the rest of my skin fell to the rooftop from my legs and feet, but the skin began to grow everywhere. The muscle tissue repaired itself. The broken bones in my ribs, the hole began to mend as the black stuff rolled off of my chest and down to my belly onto the rooftop. Little did I know, it dissolved into the roof.

Over on all fours, I rolled. In agonizing pain, I thought I ought to be in. Waiting for the pain. That's when it happened the first time, the black stuff. I threw it up. I thought it would never stop. It was all over my hands and all over my knees where I was on all fours. I couldn't breathe, but I didn't feel the pain of it. I knew I was dead. Knowing that I was going to snap out of it at any time and wake up in heaven, hell, paradise, the middle of the earth, the middle of the universe. Oh God, anywhere but here.

The black stuff oozed out of my eyes and my ears and my mouth and nose. As I threw up the last bit, it came out of every

181

hole in my body, and I do mean every hole. The black stuff was everywhere. It just kept coming out of my mouth, and then all of the sudden, I threw up the last bit and was able to take in a breath. It should have felt good on my lungs, but it didn't. It didn't feel good. It didn't feel bad.

I was scared to death, not knowing who or what I was. Not knowing whether I was dead or alive. I couldn't be alive. I had just fallen ten stories straight down, was stabbed through three times completely through my torso. My head hit the steps, crushing my skull. My legs hit the outside of the stairway, breaking my legs into pieces. But there they were, mending right before my eyes as I climbed up to my knees, and then after I got up to my knees, I lifted myself up to my feet. There I stood on my feet, looking down as the wounds mended and scarred over one by one.

The black stuff disappeared into the rooftop as it drank the last bit off of my body and torso. It just dripped right down my legs right onto the roof and was absorbed and disappeared. I looked over the edge and down the way. I couldn't see for the building next to me. It was a little bit higher, and there she was a blazing.

"Oh no," I said to myself. "Not that beautiful building." It was my favorite building. But it was burnt to the ground. I loved everything about the old building. "Even the broken banister on the first floor which ended my demise," I thought.

But now I was neither alive nor dead. Death, once my enemy, was now a thing of the past. I thought to myself, "Well if I can't die, then what am I?"

After watching the fire trucks put out the buildings beside the blazing inferno, I saw them, Cave Man and his gang. They were sitting across the street down the road, perpendicular from the place they had just burnt to the ground, and as they walked off, they were laughing as they were thinking of the money they were fixing to get paid. But I could only think of the worse things for them as I watched them walk away.

I pounded my fist down on the ledge as I stood there with my arm propped up against the side. I only thought the worst for them. "You'll get what's coming to you."

I had no clothes. Everything was burnt to a crisp. My old leather shoes fell off into pieces as I walked across the roof. Down the steps I went. Over to the fire escape I went. About four stories down. I jumped over to the next fire escape on the next building, across a pipe, and took the ladder way down from the fire escape across the alley and into a window. I went into the stairway of the building where I lived.

When I got to my apartment where we lived, I walked in. It was not a good sight. I won't talk of my family life, the abuse, the abusers. I just went to my bedroom after hearing some sharp words, not really knowing what was said. After throwing some clothes on and looking in the mirror, I was bald. My hair was completely gone, my eyebrows, my eyelashes, everything. There was no hair on my body at all, and I was scarred from one end to the other.

I don't know who it was at the door, a mom, a dad, an aunt, an uncle, legal guardians, who knows? "What happened to you? Answer me!" After a few curse words, of course, they banged three times on the door and said, "Why don't you answer me?" as I sat there looking in the mirror.

That's when the hair grew back on my head. At first, it was an eighth of an inch and then a quarter. After two long hours, the hair grew back on my body and the somewhat scars somewhat disappeared as if they looked years old. I didn't understand what had happened, but I knew it wasn't good. That was thirty years ago.

Now, the blood oozes out of my head onto the floor. The senator disappears. It drips and drips into the cracks on the floor, and through the insulation, and down the main beams.

It drips onto the ground. Now my rich red blood is no longer red. As the drip touches the ground, it turns black. The red blood goes down deep into the ground like nerve endings. The nerve endings go all the way uptown into the old buildings. And it begins to pound like a heartbeat.

"Exit military mode. Death mode activated...."

Other Titles By DW Beam:
(available at http://www.dwbeampublishing.com and other retailers near you.)

- The Adventures of Kimball McRyan Times are Hard
- The Adventures of Kimball McRyan Vol. 2 Times are the Hardest
- The Adventures of Kimball McRyan Vol. 3 Times are Harder
- Airport
- Planeterial
- Limonioum (Planeterial Vol. 2)
- Great Getaway

Upcoming Titles By DW Beam:

- Planeterial Lafi 3523 (Planeterial Vol. 3)
- City of Gold
- Dream Thief
- My Time In Prison
- The Executive

www.ingramcontent.com/pod-product-compliance
Lightning Source LLC
Chambersburg PA
CBHW060745180626
46818CB00002B/453